The Quiet Colours

LAUREEN BENNEFIELD

The Quiet Colours

Published by Benn Lee Wong Publishing
blwpub@shaw.ca

This is a work of fiction. Some characters and events in this book are fictitious. Any similarity to real persons, living or dead, is coincidental and not intended by the author.

Cover image by DesignBetiBup33 (No. 3650)

ISBN-13: 978-1-7751572-4-3

DEDICATION

To all the grains of sand that yearn to be pearls.

ACKNOWLEDGMENTS

Many thanks to author and teacher, Sarah Selecky, for her wonderful courses; many thanks to indie author and podcaster extraordinaire, Joanna Penn—you inspire me. Thank you also to my family, who willingly read everything I write, with special thanks to Juliana for her outstanding beta-reading skills.

A thank you shout-out also goes to Arnetta Jackson from lineuponlineservices.com for her professional editing services—you made everything I wrote sparkle.

And last, but never least, to Calvin—ever supportive—best friend and husband of mine. Thank you! I couldn't do this without you.

CHAPTER ONE

"You remind me . . . of . . . an old . . . hound dog." Henry dribbled out his words like a ketchup bottle—in globs and spatters that he smeared across his sleeve. He pointed to Finn. "I had to put mine down." And then dropped his chin in reverence. "Old Yeller had fleas."

Finn clenched his jaw. The squad room rippled with stifled snorts of laughter.

"Guess what?" Henry slurped. "You kinda remind me of a squirrel I once . . ." He drifted off and let the sentence swing like raw meat over a crocodile pit. His lips ebbed and flowed with every breath over gums that had long been deprived of teeth. The room fell silent, champing for his next word. He patted his tummy. ". . . ate."

Most days Henry struggled to remember his own name, or how to spell it: some days it was Henry with a "y" and some days it was Henri with an "i"—it seemed to depend how Cajun he was feeling. But, not today. For the pleasure of all staff, Henry declared that Finnegan Theodore Yung reminded him of a squirrel; not just any squirrel—the one he'd eaten for lunch.

Finn was a recent transfer to Rundle PD and the last thing he needed was staff snickering "Squirrel!" each time they saw him. Nicknames like Dredd, Machine Gun Kelly, or Cool Hand Luke were decent and hard-earned, but when they weren't, they smelled. And that smell took years to wash off. Lousy nicknames were like the nail fungus from eighth grade—the one that never healed. All you could do was wear socks all year long.

1

As he read through the overnight Intake Report, Finn alternated between tapping his pen on his desk and whacking it against his forehead. Somehow the whack-a-mole action made him concentrate better and forget about the itch. It also helped keep his hands occupied. His system was working until he swatted himself too hard, twisted his torso, and felt a searing pain on the top of his shoulder.

It's nothing, he told the mirror each morning, just a scratch from his rookie days when he'd ended up on the wrong end of a busted wine bottle. Thirty-seven stitches later, that *scratch* still sent him little *Just thinking of you* notes—*for fun*—like a nosebleed, or the flu, or diarrhea.

Finn adjusted his holster strap. It did the trick, but it wasn't remotely what he longed for. These were the moments when he played with the question, what would he give for the love of the right woman? *Everything*. His answer was always the same.

He'd crawled through the loss of his lover and best friend, his future bride and the mother of his unborn children. The tidal wave of emotions swamped him, and since the bench looked safer, he'd sidelined himself. Love hurt, so did abandonment, so did rejection. But what stung the most was that he never saw it coming. Finn never noticed the snake in the passenger seat. When it decided to curl around his chest and squeeze the oxygen from every corpuscle in his body, he flatlined, made breakfast, and went to work like nothing had happened. He was a dead man walking.

Now here he was in Rundle PD, eighteen months out. He wished he could say he was eighteen months *in*, but that would have to imply there'd been progress, and all he'd done was change his address. He wanted this move to be his genesis, a place where he could rebuild his life—by the day, the week, the month. Finn's younger sister told him, *this time it'll be different; this place will be the charm.*

He hoped she was right because it irritated him to keep chewing on that same piece of cud, inside and out; because whenever he did, the skin on his neck resembled that of a plucked goose. Or worse, like the pictures he'd seen of a group of kids swimming in Rundle's Pond after the ducks moulted. About a billion parasites had crawled into their pores and died. Try as he might to ignore those pictures and this itch, his resistance was short-lived. He dug in and scratched beneath his collar. *"Squirrel!"*

In the meantime, *Poison* Ivy's Laundry over in Rouge Market Square was off limits. The store owners must have seen the humour when somebody scratched *poison* in front of their business name, or the change increased profits. Either way, it gave Finn a solid excuse for the rash—better *poison ivy* than fleas. He pinned his free, scratching hand beneath one leg and brought his attention back to the overnight report. It gave the following details:

> *Deceased male, elderly, pierced by a sharp object inferior to the right clavicle; severed right subclavian artery; no sign of blood loss at the scene. Preliminary findings suggest someone moved the body post-mortem.*
>
> *An area sweep failed to recover a weapon, although the remnants of a broken bottle of Jamaican white rum were located. Other incidentals found at the scene: one female toddler's shoe (left, size 7, orange in colour), and a newspaper clipping advertising a two-for-the-price-of-one tire deal at a local garage.*

It was less than nothing to work with; Houdini had more. The old Finnegan would have thrown his hands in the air and brayed like a fool donkey. Only he would have used words a lot more colourful than donkey. He tilted his head back and whispered, "Kill me now."

The new Finn no longer recognized that bereft human being. He wasn't sure he'd ever known him, or liked him, but maybe for the first time in his life he was authentic. Finn closed the file and flipped it into the tray labelled *Intake Reports*. The basket was already many inches high—new and pending cases piling up by the hour. He let out a loathsome sigh; he'd been on the job for a week.

At the far end of the squad room stood a steel cage designated as a temporary holding cell. The only witness to this case of indecent human disposal and possible homicide was also doubling as the only suspect. He stretched to see past a sleeping Henry and watched this caged suspect with a renewed interest.

Miss Newman, witness and murder suspect, sat expressionless. In fact, she hadn't stirred once in the past hour. She presided over her cell space like a vintage barrel of one-hundred-year-old brandy up for auction: every dram was going to cost you—big time.

But there was also a softness to her and Finn felt impelled to picture her as a lioness. It was easy to imagine her surrounded by a litter of cubs, all clamouring for her attention as they pulled on her tail and chomped on her ears. She purred and licked clean her sharp claws, untroubled by those frisky cubs. She only took exception when one cub tangled itself in the lavender-coloured scarf draped around her muscular neck.

Without warning, the fatigued springs in Finn's old chair recoiled. He snapped forward into the desk, catching himself seconds before he wore a full cup of coffee. Finn jerked his arm toward the woman and yelled, "Simpson! Get that scarf out of lockup."

Simpson sucked his belly back into the coffee room. He looked toward the ceiling, searching for a glimmer of hope in the brown-stained tiles, then shook his head. He had predicted this was coming and had promised himself he'd make it right—just not right this minute. He took a swig and hid the flask in his trousers, muttering about the injustice of it all. Simpson poked his head through the doorway, followed this time by a steaming mug of coffee in one hand and a maple-glazed donut in the other.

"I already tried." He sputtered as he swallowed the donut whole without so much as a bite mark. Simpson had one plan of escape: choke to death on his donut; make Finn so caught up in saving him, that he forgot about the scarf.

Finn read Sonny's face and shook his head.

Sonny "Santino" Simpson fancied himself a player and a lady's man. His long, dark lashes and blue eyes were a never-ending magnet for trouble. He was a robust man with eighteen solid years on the force. And although he'd ventured more to the portly side of robust these past few years, Sonny remained a valued officer, claiming last year's Medal of Valour Award.

It was rumoured that his swagger alone could unsettle most hardened criminals and had made more than a few young women go weak in the knees. Today, that was ancient history, because today Sonny "Santino" Simpson hit the wall, and he hit it hard. Faced with this enemy, he conceded defeat. He set his coffee on Finn's desk and shook the remaining donut bits from his necktie. He rolled up his sleeve and showed Finn the teeth marks on his forearm.

"For Pete's sake, she's a middle-aged woman!"

Finn's voice startled Henry awake just long enough for him

to join the conversation and share a little forty-proof advice. "Sometimes, it's just more *human* to shoot 'em."

"Careful, Henry, before somebody shoots you." Sonny flicked him on the ear as he guided his wobbly steps to Booking.

"All's I'm saying is that maybe she's *rabbit*." His eyes got big.

"It's *rabid*. And, she's not." Sonny seized him by the shoulders and gave him a firm shake. "I don't want to see you end up like that frozen old stiff they brought in here last night. He had nobody looking out for him." Henry nodded and stumbled toward his cell. Sonny shut the door and watched the old man curl up on his bunk.

He tapped his signet ring against the bars. "What's on the breakfast menu?"

"Puffed Wheat and milk."

Sonny made a gag reflex.

"Cut backs." The guard shrugged.

He opened his wallet and removed a $10 bill. "Make sure Henry gets an omelette, OJ and whole wheat toast—no bacon, though; he'd be gumming that until tomorrow night." He turned on his heels and headed back toward the squad room.

"You know he's never going to change."

Sonny kept walking. "He might."

"You said that the last time." The guard laughed and pocketed the $10.

****

Across the room, a pair of amber-coloured eyes tracked Finn's every move. He stooped low, pretending to tie a shoelace and peered over the wire mesh of his wastebasket. There she was; watching him, watching her. He tugged at his tie and undid his collar. It felt good to let his inflamed pores breathe; later he'd smother them to death with some Calamine lotion.

Finn marched up to the holding cell and clanged the door open; he was a man on a mission. Miss Newman was a mystery: was she an exotic burl or a formidable lioness hunting a gazelle on the African savanna? Finn didn't need a crystal ball to deduce she was not the cold-blooded killer of an elderly man, but then again, what did he know—a flea-infested, love-forsaken rodent—a squirrel.

He held out his hand and asked for the scarf. She uncoiled it from her neck and let it dance to the floor. "Remember, detective, I'll be getting that back."

This lioness was no longer playing with her cubs; she was toying with a squirrel. She locked eyes with Finn as he retreated, scarf in hand. He closed the cell door and gave it an extra tug for good measure.

CHAPTER TWO

Over at The Milky Way Convenience store, parents jostled one another to claim the few remaining treats while the darkening streets of Rundle's Landing were already lined with little Groots, and ghouls, and goblins. With half-empty bags in hand, parents hurried home to put supper on the table and face the indignant looks of their children.

"What?"

"It was all they had."

"No one will notice."

"Okay, fine. Give me some of your candy. Come on! Your bag's overflowing!"

Children were subjected to the same rerun every Halloween: it starred parents who should have skipped the day and stayed in bed. In plain language, it was embarrassing—ask any one of their kids.

****

"Mom? Ben and I are heading out." Truebell called to her from beneath a mop of dark curls that hung past his eyebrows. His jeans rode higher on his ankles than he liked, but his mom teased that they matched his t-shirts, some barely making it to his waistband. Such were the realities for gangly teenage boys—nothing fit for long.

Once upon a time, True had been the proud son of Harper and Reggie. Now he belonged to her. Life circumstances had cancelled his status as son and replaced it with a new title, "man of the house." It happened in a single raindrop on a slippery stretch of road and no one even thought to ask for his permission.

Sydney was his little sister and Ben was his best friend. And when his world toppled, first with his dad and then with Sydney, he learned that nothing was sacred; everything changes.

"Be home by 10:00."

There was a loud grunt, marked by a few incoherent grumbles. "How does 9:30 sound? Any better . . .?" she raised her voice and waited for an argument.

"Fine . . ." The door slammed shut. Harper exhaled. It was all she needed to say. The boy was full up on black marks and one more would cancel his winter ski trip.

Streetlights were just coming to life. It was that mysterious, between-worlds time of day when common sense was replaced with the thrill of the hunt. The boys settled on a game plan and headed east toward Opal Meadows—better snatch-and-grab opportunities than the west end of town.

Ben pulled out the two cigarettes he'd swiped from his older brother's pack. He tucked one behind his ear and offered True the other. "Want a smoke?"

"No, Sydney's asthma acts up around cigarette smoke." Sydney was three; the miracle baby. He would never jeopardize that.

"Doesn't your mom smoke?"

"Not anymore."

Ben laughed and punched True in the arm, "And not any less!"

"You're such a tool . . ."

"What? You always laugh at that . . ."

They walked a few steps in silence before True swung his leg around behind and clipped Ben on his skinny butt. "Okay, it was funny."

The boys looked up as Cynthia Dowd, the bodacious offspring of Debbie Dowd, rounded the corner ahead of them. Ben yelled, "Yo, *Harley Quinn*! Looking good!" He grinned and clucked his tongue against the roof of his mouth. His cigarette fell on the ground.

Cynthia swung her bat behind her back, caught it with her free hand and cracked her spine. Then she raised it over her head and loosened her hips. Limbered up, she stepped into an imaginary batter's box and tapped her bat against each heel. "Goodnight, boys." They backed up; in awe and a little in fear.

True looked at Cynthia and sighed. She looked like a hot

science experiment gone wickedly right. Somewhere a secret lab had squeezed her into a *Daddy's Lil Monster* t-shirt and a pair of black fishnet stockings. Ben opened his mouth to drool just as Cynthia blew a bubble: a large, pink one. She popped it with a resounding crack.

"Easy, pubes . . ."

It was Wyatt, Cynthia's boyfriend, dressed as the Joker. He had slicked back lime-green hair and teeth capped with aluminum foil. His strides were long and steady: about four feet. Wyatt was the Bluenose; sails unfurled, setting out to sea. With arms swinging high in his grandfather's old topcoat, he gave each boy a *thwack* on the head as he steamed by.

"I don't think you're ready for the likes of her," he said with a hearty laugh as he plucked the remaining cigarette from behind Ben's ear.

Ben scrambled to all fours and searched for the smoke he'd dropped. He found it and showed True: a crumpled tube of paper and tobacco. "I must have stepped on it." He kicked it to the side of the road.

True snorted. "What does he know? *"I don't think you're ready for the likes of her, yet!"*

"Do you think he'll smoke it, or throw it away?"

"Have you heard anything I said?"

"Sure. Wyatt knows you still wet the bed. And, he didn't say *yet*, so I'm pretty sure he meant *never*." Ben took off running, filling the night with his laughter.

CHAPTER THREE

"Ready to go, Sydney?" Harper gave Frankenstein a big smile.

"Mommy, your tooth's all black!"

"And you have puppy dog ears and a kitty tail."

"Don't forget my ducky toes . . ." She pointed to the yellow plastic webbing that encased each foot.

The black-toothed tramp picked up a small burlap bundle tied with a red handkerchief, anchored it to a stick, and swung it over her shoulder. She had donned an old pair of Reggie's work trousers and completed the look with a belt made of twine and one of his flannel shirts that substituted as a nightgown on cold or lonely nights.

"Okay, Frankie, let's go get us some candy!"

"Yeah!" Sydney jumped up and down in her assorted animal parts. Her eyes grew wide and she squeezed her knees together. "I has to pee."

Ten minutes later, Harper plopped Sydney back into her stroller and wheeled her down the driveway.

"Giddy up, Ho!" Sydney commanded.

"That's hobo to you, young lady!"

"That's not what Ben said when he comed to pick up Toobell."

Harper was huffing as she ran the stroller up the steep incline toward Greystone Boulevard. "And what did your brother say?"

"Nuffing."

"Nothing . . . ?"

"Nope. He punched him. Hard."

Harper beamed and erased one black mark from True's list. *No,* she softened, *let's make it two.* She took a cleansing breath and chugged forward.

****

"Harper? Harper Steele? Is that you?"

A woman with blonde sprigs of hair poking out from beneath her hairnet frantically waved from the house across the street. Her full, pouty lips were a deep vermilion colour that matched her gel fingernails.

Her eyelids glistened azure blue from the base of her false eyelashes to her thinly pencilled half-brows, beginning about mid-pupil and carrying on in a sweeping, upturned broad stroke to the edge of her natural eye. On top of this woolly nimbus, perched a brown cap with a pumpkin-orange stripe. She was the total package, an A&W Halloween-diva.

"Heh, Debbie." Harper eased her pace to a full stop. Her chest was heaving and her breaths were ragged.

"Where's the fire, girl?" Debbie Dowd boomed into her wireless headset as she skated across the street. She wore white derby-style roller skates to complement her vintage carhop uniform, carried a serving tray loaded down with candy, and an authentic coin-dispensing machine cinched to her waist. Debbie harrumphed. People *strolled* by her house at a leisurely pace: they gazed, they admired her effort and fine attention to detail—they did not run by—sweaty and out of breath.

"It's Salmon."

"What is?"

"My last name."

"Oh? Wouldn't you rather use your maiden name? Now . . .?" Debbie sounded baffled.

"No. It's the last name of my children."

"Well, isn't that just wonderful!" Debbie gushed.

"That my children have the same last name?"

"Oh, hon, no need to explain. You and I go way back. Remember?" She opened her mouth as if to say *duh.* "I just figured enough time had passed, and you were putting yourself back in the butcher's display case."

"Now I'm a rack of lamb?"

"Heavens, no! That's much too big of a stretch for you.

Lambs are for spring time relations, if you know what I mean."
Debbie rolled her eyes. "You may still be able to catch a pot roast.
But if you're going to walk around presenting yourself like chipped
beef on toast . . ." She gave Harper a dismissive *I've got nothing for you*
gesture.

Harper let the comments slide. It was high school all over
again: Debbie was a senior and the head cheerleader; Harper was just
a freshman and never good enough to make the *Debbie-list*. She knelt
beside the stroller and fished out a juice box for Sydney.

"Well, those are cute." Debbie stretched out the word for
emphasis as she tugged on Sydney's ears. She circled the stroller:
debating, analyzing, critiquing, and then jammed in for a closer look.

"Careful, Debbie, the dentist discovered an extra row of teeth
on her last checkup." It was a joke—sort of. Little Sydney was a
known biter; the daycare had posted her photo on their Wall of
Shame, right next to the Post Office's Most Wanted list. Harper
sighed. She warned people: *If you like having five fingers on each hand, don't
stick them near Sydney's face.*

Debbie yanked back her hand and tucked it into one of her
uniform pockets. "True out trick or treating this year?"

"Yes, he is."

"Huh?" She snorted. "I told Cynthia on no uncertain terms
could she go out this year—she's practically a senior. What would
the best people say if they saw her?"

"It's doubtful I know any." Harper chuckled. "By the way,
isn't Cynthia a junior—same as True?"

"To/ma/to, to/mat/o." Debbie smiled. "It's all the same."

She changed the subject and stroked Sydney's fluffy tail. It
curled around her back and then draped itself adorably over one side
of the stroller; it dared anyone to pet it. *Fool me twice? I don't think so,
Franken-baby!* Debbie rolled her fingers into a fist and eased herself
away from the danger zone.

Before Debbie rolled completely out of reach, the monster
baby spoke, "Candy?" Her pink, pudgy tentacles crept toward the
tray of candy in search of the black licorice tucked beneath the
mound of Little Debbie treats. Sydney pulled out three packets and
secured them in her kangaroo pouch.

"Thanking you." She gave a double wink to her mom and
smiled up at Debbie.

Debbie returned the smile. It was dental-visit wide and unnatural, showing a half-dozen teeth with silver amalgam fillings in the back and two teeth in the front leaking blood-red lipstick. Sydney looked back and forth from Harper's blacked out teeth to Debbie's diseased mouth. She wrinkled her brow as she tried to remember. "Mommy's a . . . a homo, too."

"That's hobo, baby. Ho—bo," Harper choked out the words.

It was too late, Debbie had already skated back to her side of the street where the lights were pretty and everybody played her game. "It's not like I need some sticky-fingered three-year-old starting rumours about me!"

"You can't be serious?"

"*Serious!*" She screeched. "Listen, Harper Steele, or whatever you call yourself, I know for a fact you're still upset that my Bill took Reggie's job away from him."

"Reggie's dead—almost three years now. His job could have gone to anyone."

Debbie shook her finger. "But it didn't. It went to my Bill and that irks you. Plus, I have a husband and you don't. Plus, I've done a great job raising my daughter; while you—you let yours almost drown."

Harper's mouth fell open.

Debbie lurched to a stop at the bottom of her stairs and roller-bumped up to the veranda, hissing at an empty house.

Sydney's eyes were round and glassy. She reached for Harper's hand.

"It's okay; she's just having a bad day." Harper collected Sydney's empty juice box and returned it to the snack bag. She leaned in and kissed her baby's wet cheek.

"If I remember correctly, she was born having a bad day—"

Harper's lip quivered when she spotted Mr. Weaver climbing down his step ladder. She'd been so caught up in Debbie's vitriol, she'd forgotten all about the one person with ringside tickets to every show in the neighbourhood.

The large maple tree was his favourite post. He swayed for hours on the branch that hung directly over his front sidewalk. From here he monitored the neighbourhood, and far beyond—on a clear night. Every Halloween he'd slowly lower furry black widow spiders on fishing line and wait for the screams, much to the chagrin of his one and only daughter, Debbie Dowd. It never got old for him.

Harper flushed. "I don't understand her anger."

"It's not you." He reassured her. "There's a rumour going around that *her Bill* is having an affair."

"I'm sorry, I hadn't heard. Do you know who she is?"

"There's the rub, Harper. She thinks it's you."

"I'm not—I wouldn't."

Mr. Weaver adjusted his trousers. They liked to hike up around his armpits anytime he climbed down from his tree. He'd been holding off ordering a pair of acrobatic leotards, fearing someone might refer to them as yoga pants. Now, with Harper standing directly in front of him, he realized he may have waited too long.

"Not to worry, she'll figure that out soon enough." He gave one final tug on the front of his pants and a quick adjustment in the rear. Harper seemed not to take notice; she kept her eyes trained on Debbie's house.

"I hope you're right about that." She looked deflated. "Is he really having an affair?"

"No." Mr. Weaver snickered. "My daughter would much rather believe her husband is cheating rather than accept he's getting down and dirty with a bowling ball."

The tramp took a firm grip on baby Frankenstein's stroller and pushed off beyond the edges of light to the shadows. In a way, it relieved her to leave behind one crazed woman holed up in her house; one quirky man wearing snug-fitting khaki pants who liked to spend his time holed up in a tree; and one sign that read: *Beware! There be dragons here!*

Mr. Weaver waved until he could barely make out the faintest outline of an arm waving back; a heaviness settled on his chest. Looking down the road, he counted three discarded packets of candy: unopened and unwanted. He walked over and picked them up, then reached down once more and selected three nice-sized chunks of gravel and threw them at his daughter's house. It was satisfying to envision a jumbo-sized crack in her plate-glass window . . . but he'd settle for a nick.

When none of the rocks hit their mark, he breathed a sigh of relief. Although, one did bounce off her white metal hand railing, and that made him feel better—a little "David" vindication against

Harper's "Goliath." Debbie stuck her head out the front door just as her father turned his back on her.

Mr. Weaver climbed the rungs of his old wooden ladder and cloistered himself in the tree. He gave her a loving pat. This tree—he had named her Eloise—knew all his secrets, all his dreams. She was his best friend. He wondered if she knew how or why things had gone sideways with his daughter—and his wife. If she knew, she never said; she just supported him through it all.

CHAPTER FOUR

Opal Meadows still lay two blocks ahead and already the boys were only steps away from the grandeur, the shininess of wealth, and the trendy, reusable, designer poop bags.

"How much longer are you Halloweening?"

"It's only 8:30, man. We're good for time." Ben furrowed his brow and read the time on his Fitbit.

Truebell suddenly felt very old. "Yeah, you're right—let's make history this year—epic history."

They hung back on the sidewalk for a few minutes, waiting for a group of parents with young children to leave. The target: a dimly lit, brick, Tudor-styled house near the wooded parkway. When the last group raced off, they crept up the walkway. Ben raised a stick he'd picked up a few blocks earlier and let it bump against the doorbell.

"Remind me why we come here every year?" Clumps of yellow-green bile inched up the back of his throat. He swallowed hard.

"It's cool. This year things will be different." Ben gave him a friendly shove. "Just follow my lead."

"What lead?" True wheezed. "You never lead."

"You'll see."

Everett Moore swung open the double oak doors and leaned against the frame. With a shake of his head, he tossed back a few strands of yellow-blonde hair and arched an eyebrow.

"Hey, Sneverett," Ben greeted him with a fist bump. Everett

ignored it.

"Well, well, well, who do we have here? Tweedle Pee and Tweedle Pooh?"

True pointed at his golf knickers. "I don't know, Caddyshack, you tell us?"

"You're rather cocky for a kid with one parent."

"Why do you have to be such a turd, Moore?"

"What?" Everett whined, clutching his heart while he batted his eyelids. "Can't a guy kid around with his friends?"

True turned to leave. "We're not friends."

Everett held up the goody bag. "Come on. Benny, True—have some candy . . ."

He plucked two mini M&Ms from an open packet and tossed a single candy into the face of each boy. "What's the problem? I let my butt lick them first."

He smartly did an *about-face* and demonstrated, then extended an arm into the hallway and found his old girlfriend leaning against the wall. His hand slid down her graphite shaft as he snaked her through the doorway. She glinted under the porch light; her gigantic melon head still dripping with the remnants of past foes. Everett spread his feet shoulder-width apart—eyes down—and lined up the enemy's head with his best girl: Big Bertha.

"Fore!"

The camcorder's red light continued to blink off and on. "Cut! Cut!"

Everett lowered his weapon. "What now, Fraser?" He glared at his younger brother.

True and Ben were prostrate on the lawn, gripping blades of grass with their nose hairs. Fraser did a quick sweep up and down the street for any adult witnesses, and then jerked his fingers toward the two teenage boys growing out of the lawn where none had been moments earlier.

"What do you think it could be?" He clenched his fist. "Idiot!"

Everett giggled. "Is it because they look like a couple of trashy garden gnomes—like always?"

"No! It's because you're acting like someone who's off his meds!" Fraser pushed his skinny frame up against his brother's and then scurried inside.

"Well, at least I'm *on* meds!" Everett hurled Big Bertha into the neighbour's flowerbed. "Now, look what you made me do, Fraser!" He stomped into the house after his brother and slammed the double doors with a resounding thud.

Minutes passed before True hoisted himself off the ground. As he did, the left door cracked open a sliver and Fraser's thin face peered through; he quickly tossed out five large bags of Skittles, two bags of Twizzlers, and a $20. He took a second glance at True's stunned face; he dug into his pocket and added a crumpled $10 to the mix.

The door closed again—this time with the added sound of multiple tumblers locking into place—jarring the uneasy silence. The porch lights blinked off and left them standing in the dark, surrounded by a heap of candy and a couple of bills.

"No hard feelings?" Ben held out his hand.

True swatted his hand away. "Let me guess, credit for your drama class with Fraser?" He grabbed the $20 and both bags of Twizzlers.

Ben started to protest and then noticed the front of True's pants. "Don't get mad, but I think your jeans are crying . . ."

"This is my last Halloween." He untucked his shirt, hoping it might cover his pants and knowing it wouldn't. "I have no dignity left."

"And you think I do?"

"Just tell me why you always set me up: for junk food, for money?" He threw the licorice and the $20 at him.

Ben was silent.

"Oh, brother, don't give me that. There's only one victim here and you're staring at his pants."

Ben's earlier bravado was gone. "Fraser promised he'd set up a date for me."

"Set up a *what?*"

"A date—with Cynthia."

"And you believed him?"

It was a clear night and as True gazed up at the Big Dipper, its handle slowly rotating to the icicle position. He knew winter was coming. He looked over at Ben—all this—over a girl? Cynthia Dowd wasn't even his type; she was tangy sriracha to Ben's milk toast.

The corners of his mouth relaxed and he put his arm around Ben. "You were hosed, buddy."

Ben scuffed his runners on the grass. "I know."

True checked his watch and headed off down the street. He had just enough time to get home before his curfew.

"No!" Ben grabbed him by the collar and turned him toward Onyx Ave. "Okay, I admit this was a bust, but *trust* me—you don't want to miss what's coming next. I've already done the recon work. We can't lose."

True anchored his feet to the ground. "Trust *me*, Benjamin, I'm not moving until you trade pants with me."

CHAPTER FIVE

Terri Newman rocked in her chair, gently dabbing the perspiration that had collected in her cleavage. Without a Mr. Newman, she was on her own for all the heavy, so-called, *man work,* which she never minded unless the heat was smoldering. Unfortunately, the entire month of October had been smoldering.

It's always nice to offer folks something cool on a hot night, Terri Lynne. Her mother's words swirled in her ears like the bits of freshly squeezed lemons in the glasses of iced tea and lemonade she had set out. Terri missed her parents most keenly at this time of the year.

When they died, it was the end of her legacy. There was no one left to tell that Terri had ever been part of something normal and loving, like a family. Their deaths swallowed up her former life, inch by inch, just like the soil that covered their coffins. This Terri, the one who slowly rocked in her chair, was the result of an unnatural creation, but she'd made the best of it. There was no other choice.

Terri was primed, ready for the first trick or treaters to arrive—even that wretched feline, Quigley. He was the neighbourhood cat who liked to jump onto the railing that traversed her veranda. And each time he did, it was a tossup who hissed the loudest. But there was no contest about who hightailed it away the quickest. *Triumphant, again,* Terri beamed as Quigley raced for cover in the underbrush.

She smoothed her skirt and returned to the gentle rhythm of the chair: back and forth, back and forth. The motion was hypnotic and soon her heavy lids closed. From a distance, it was difficult to tell if she was actually alive, or a decoy. She looked like one of those automated mannequins designed to jump up and scare supper right out of you. And she preferred it that way.

Terri was a newcomer to Rundle's Landing with barely three months under her girdle; she was an acquired taste for the locals, and they to her. But Halloween was her favourite holiday and she prided herself on having the best lawn display on the block. She had a Keeper of the Crypt, dismembered bodies strewn about, and her own grave marker:

> *Here laid Miss Terri Newman*
> *People thought she was dead, or so they said.*
> *But when they buried her deep in that frozen sleep,*
> *She thawed and gnawed and clawed her way out.*

She loved and hated that sign because it told the story of her life.

CHAPTER SIX

When Harper had put a little distance between herself and Debbie, she had to admit the encounter was laughable, at least she hoped it would be in about fifty years. Maybe it was something her great-grandchildren would enjoy hearing about.

She closed her eyes and set the scene: white-haired, wire-frame spectacles balancing on the tip of her nose, a hand-knit sweater, and a calico cat upon her lap. She'd hush the children gathered at her feet and begin the tale with, *Once upon a spooky eve*. She'd describe the red-fanged, hair-sprigging, blue-eyed monster on wheels; the fearsome, trans-animal, girl-creature in the transportation buggy; and end with the enchanting guardian hobo angel who saved the day.

"Oh, Frankie, Mommy needs to teach you about words."

Sydney nodded. "OK, but more candy first."

"You got it. Let's head over to Grandma and Grandpa's." Sydney made a face.

"Why the look?"

"Grandpa gives out tooth brushes," she assured her mother. "He told me last night."

Harper did her best to look surprised.

"Yes, and he's gonna be mad at you because you wasted all the money he and Grandma paid to fix your crooked teeth." She opened her own mouth to show Harper which of her teeth had rotted since this morning.

"It's not good news for you." Sydney shook her head.

"Well, maybe we can see them tomorrow. I'm betting my teeth will look a thousand times better after a good night's sleep." She smiled.

"That would be a miracle."

"Then that's two miracles for me."

Sydney snuggled into her mother's arms. She knew this word, though the memory of it was fading. Sydney squeezed her eyes tight and allowed herself to float like she was in the bathtub—it was there she could still feel the magic. Then, like a dog without a bone, she was off memory lane and back on the Halloween train track: candy, candy, and more candy.

Except, for one last question . . .

"Did you call *Toobell, Toobell,* 'cause he's trouble?"

Harper hadn't thought about Truebell's name for years. It was just a matter of record. Like something sewn into the fabric of their family that she never questioned. But Sydney was right, even with a three-year-old's understanding: Truebell was always in trouble and without his dad to offer guidance . . . Harper shook her head. *Who was she kidding,* she thought. She missed Reggie, too: his abominable sense of humour, his appetite for life, for love, for her. Harper had tried to convince herself that Sydney was the lucky one—how could she miss what she'd never known? She looked down at Sydney—her little girl's eyes wise beyond their years. Suddenly, she wasn't so sure.

"Speaking of your brother, maybe we'd better head back. How will it look if he beats us home?"

"Oh, Harper, you funny."

"*Now* you're calling me Harper?"

"You didn't like Ho, 'member?"

Those were the golden threads of their conversation as they retraced their steps through Greystone Boulevard and into Rosewood cul-de-sac—the place they called home.

****

It was nearing 9:30 and Sydney was too tired to put up much of a struggle when Harper tucked her into bed. "Goodnight, love bug. Don't let the bedbugs bite."

She finished her mother's sentence and giggled. "Only me."

Harper stepped outside and listened for the sounds of two raucous boys making their way home. Silence. She snuffed out the lit pumpkins and moved them away from the steps and closer to the house. No point tempting fate, or teenagers high on sugar, or worse.

She could see the lights of Debbie's house shining through the neighbour's yard. It looked more like a Friday night football game than a spooky bungalow decorated for Halloween. Harper caught herself laughing out loud thinking about Debbie's father, Mr. Weaver, reposed in the maple tree with his binoculars and his bunched-up khaki's.

Inside the house, her kettle sang. Within minutes, she sat down to enjoy a steaming cup of chai tea. The second hand clicked to 9:45.

"Come on, True." Harper's fingers danced on the table.

****

True pointed at his watch. "Ben! I can't be late again. Get going."

"Shh! You'll wake her."

The boys had staked out Terri Newman's house. She appeared to be fast asleep on her front porch, surrounded by a table lined with frosted glasses and a tray of candy—ready for the taking.

"It's ours." It was as if all the stars had aligned for Benjamin.

"I don't like the looks of it. Who's that guy leaning against the tree?"

"What guy?"

Truebell raised a finger in the direction of the dummy in the black suit. "I think he's melting."

"No, that's spray from the sprinklers. He's just part of the setup—he's the Crypt Keeper."

"All I know is that I have seven minutes to get home. If you're going to do something—do it now."

Ben scampered up the steps and slammed back a glass of iced tea. Next, he grabbed the tray of goodies, swooped over the railing, and landed on the walkway. He did his best victory yelp and headed for the Promised Land.

****

"Not a moment to spare, Truebell." Harper called her son by his given name as she showed him her wrist watch. She had returned to her mom role and donned a pair of faded jeans and a sleeveless cotton top. Her hair was piled up in a lazy top knot—some may have called it bedhead—but she didn't care.

Caught up in all the drama, she'd forgotten about the black electrician tape on her teeth. Ben covered his mouth and pretended to cough.

"I know it's warm right now," she handed them extra blankets and smiled, "but by morning there'll be icicles hanging from your nose hair." Her two young men, so boyishly handsome, standing on the precipice of manhood. Ready to jump if she blinked. *It's all happening so fast*, she told herself. *So fast.*

"Oh, sure . . ." They tried to look anywhere but her mouth.

"Okay then." She gave them a sleepy yawn and headed off to bed.

****

True flipped on the Coleman lantern as they rolled onto the sleeping bags, howling at Harper's black teeth.

"How does she do it?" Ben snorted.

"Do what?"

"Keep a straight face while smiling with those blacked teeth?"

"Oh, that . . . she's a real kidder."

"I'd trade you any day of the week." Ben lay back on his pillow.

"Don't be thinking like that about my mom!" True tossed a bag of Skittles at his head.

"I'm not . . . I'm just missing mine." Ben's mom and dad were divorced and according to the court, Ben won the lottery—he got to live with his dad fulltime and learn to walk on eggshells. His mom never contested the decision. He said it didn't matter.

Silence passed between them for a moment and then it was back to black teeth, Miss Terri Newman, and surviving Everett Moore.

"What a score!" Ben roared as he bounced the spoils from the night off the tent walls.

"Go to sleep!" Harper roared even louder from her bedroom window. Peals of laughter continued; their faces pressed hard into their pillows; then more sporadic fits and starts until the silent pauses grew and a deep, restful sleep had overtaken them.

CHAPTER SEVEN

At a quarter past twelve, sirens wailed through Rundle's Landing as they sped toward Onyx Avenue. Mr. Weaver was the first one to his window. Thirty years on the Fire Department had sensitized him to the particular sound of sirens. He listened closely and switched on his police scanner for details. Sure enough, someone had called in a report about a drunken man accosting a woman on her front lawn. Mr. Weaver dug out the map for Rundle's Landing and determined the location.

"Bingo!"

His finger drew a line from his home, through his daughter's home, the Vickers' who lived behind Debbie, through Harper's home and—*Voilà!* He headed out to the front yard, climbed his ladder, and attached his night vision goggles. The gentle downward slope of the land was perfect and so was his line of sight.

"Halloween, the gift that keeps on giving . . ." He got comfortable. *Maybe it's a takedown*, he mused, giddy as a school boy.

****

"True, turn off the lantern!" Ben barked the order through a sleepy haze.

"Quiet! It's the cops!"

"What'd you do?"

"Me?!" True blinked in disbelief. "You're the one who stole the candy and wrecked the iced tea!" True opened the tent flaps a little for Ben to see out. "See? The cops are at Miss Newman's. Maybe you frightened her to death?"

26

"No way! She nearly ripped off my shirt." Ben showed him the tears in the fabric and the missing buttons.

"Well, you did something . . ." True examined his shirt. "Those buttons were missing when you got here."

"Boys!" Harper stood there framed by the moonlight; a ghostly apparition wielding a flashlight and a toy croquet mallet. They fell backwards into the tent.

"Come inside. I don't know what's going on over there, but you two needn't get involved." She snapped her fingers. "Double time. Let's go."

The boys scrambled from the tent and ran to the house. True glanced back for his mom and watched her walk off toward the rear gate of their property. "Mom! Where are you going?"

"To check on Miss Newman."

"You don't even know her! It could be . . . dangerous."

"Don't be silly. She's our neighbour." Harper paused at the gate. "True?"

"*Yes?*" It was a high-pitched nervous response. He cleared his throat and tried again. "Yes?"

"Make up the spare bedroom, please. I've a feeling she may need a place to stay."

****

Squad cars lined the front of Miss Newman's house. It was unmistakable that there'd been a scuffle: smashed iced tea and lemonade glasses littered the porch and sticky liquid dripped everywhere. Terri's RIP sign had a boot print stomped on it and the "No Trespassing" sign had been completely destroyed. As Harper rounded the giant blue spruce trees, she found Miss Newman seated on a plastic folding chair—in restraints.

"Is that necessary?" She gasped and looked to a neighbour for validation.

"Oh, yes, Harper! She's a wild one." The woman tightened the grip she had on her robe.

"And, is that a body?" Harper felt sickened. A yellow bag was laid out on the lawn and something zippered up inside.

"Folks, it's time to go home! This is a crime scene: police business only." The officer with the bullhorn squawked out the orders, getting up close and personal with those who were slow to obey.

"That means you, too, ma'am." He stopped in front of Harper.

"Of course." She headed back to her yard.

"Whoa, whoa, whoa! Where do you think you're going?"

"Home?" She pointed toward her house where two boys watched from beneath the porch light—illuminated for the officer to see. "I live that way."

"Those are *your* sons?"

"One of them; the other is his friend."

"And they were out earlier?"

"Yes." Her voice was losing its usual friendliness as she flipped back some hair using the end of Sydney's mallet. "Is there a problem?"

"Miss Newman? Are those the two boys who ransacked your display?" He directed her attention up the rise to Harper's house.

Miss Newman peered past Harper. "I can't be sure."

"Could you be sure if I removed your restraints?"

She glanced at Harper, standing there with a heavy-duty MagLight in one hand and a pink toy mallet in the other. It was an odd combination, but Terri admired her courage. Calling out two young scoundrels would be the normal thing to do, but it wasn't the Terri Newman thing.

"No."

The officer grunted and turned to address Harper, "My apologies, ma'am. You're free to leave."

She hesitated. "Miss Newman, my name's Harper Salmon. I live right behind you." She indicated her house using the mallet. "Is there something I can do to help?"

Terri held up her zip-locked wrists. "Too late."

****

When the last police car pulled away, Mr. Weaver removed his goggles, yawned and wrestled his back into place with a few, careful twists. It was enough excitement for one night. He clambered down the ladder and rested for a moment against his tree—Harper and her *boys* could wait for the morning.

"Goodnight, old girl." He patted her trunk and shuffled to his house.

CHAPTER EIGHT

The month of November dawned with the usual streaks of blue and magenta, a few low-lying clouds threatening a change in the weather, but with no more clarity than the night before.

"So, who's the dead guy?" Sonny rolled up his sleeves. He was eager to get this case solved. "Any leads?"

"No positive ID yet, but we know he was wearing a fifty-year-old suit."

"Probably the one he got married in," said Sonny. He hadn't meant to mock the man, but it came across that way. "Poor old wretch—married and died in the same suit." Sonny ran his fingers over his silk tie and custom-made shirt.

"And the Newman woman?" He felt for her bite marks. *Probably should've had it checked—maybe get a tetanus shot; maybe rabies? No, probably should've charged her—with assault!* He shook his head.

"She exercised her right to *remain silent*. We had to let her go."

"Hasn't forensics at least determined how John Doe died?"

"Nada." Finn laughed. "The prelims were all wrong. It looks like someone kept him on ice for days, maybe weeks—the body had freezer burns. And those wounds?" This time he snorted. "They're all post-mortem."

Simpson blinked. People were not kept on ice in Rundle's Landing. "What about those two kids? I could head over and talk to the mom?" He dangled the offer, flipping his keys in and out of his palm as he waited.

The arresting officer had mentioned Harper when he'd

brought in Miss Newman. He'd also taken it upon himself to describe her in splendid moonlit detail, like some Greek goddess carrying a torch. If anyone interviewed this woman, it would not be Sonny, the silver fox, Simpson. *No, no, no,* Finn decided. He looked up. Sonny waited by his desk—a hopeful smile on his face. Finn smiled back and shook his head.

He picked up his notes and headed for Rosewood cul-de-sac. Second house on the left, two story, white with pink trim, yellow rose bushes that framed the front porch. Not that he'd looked it up on Google Earth, or anything so desperate. It was routine surveillance of the crime scene and surrounding terrain—at least that's what he told himself.

Once he stepped out of the car and inhaled the sweet scent of her roses and the fresh coffee brewing inside, he could hardly remember his own name. He held out his hand and practiced: *Hello, I'm Detective Yung; Hello, I'm Finnegan; Hello, I'm lost; Hello, Rundle PD— at your service. Call me anytime. Really—just call.*

CHAPTER NINE

Mr. Weaver overslept that first morning in November, the bands of blue and magenta in the morning sky had already turned to golden pinks. When he finally turned over and rubbed the sleep from his eyes, it was 0700. He could count the number of times the sun rose before him on one finger, and that was the day after he'd said goodbye to Mrs. Weaver.

The *unravelling*, as he liked to call it, began almost three years earlier. It was an early June morning, and he'd just gotten home after a harrowing night at work. He'd made a lettuce and tomato sandwich, mumbled a quick prayer to the patron saint of firemen, and climbed into bed—exhausted and more than a little sad. His crew had responded to a serious traffic accident involving a big rig and an SUV. It had happened on Hwy 53, a few kilometers north of town.

Rain fell heavy that day and well into the evening. The roads were slick. Later, when police interviewed the truck driver, he said it was like dancing on gorilla snot. He said he was headed around the bend that slopes down to Rundle's Landing when his trailer "greased" over the white line. The SUV never stood a chance. The truck's trailer careened over the SUV and compacted the roof onto the driver. Fire & Rescue responded with the jaws of life equipment and Mr. Weaver wedged himself beside the driver; holding his hand, never letting it go. It was plain to see there wasn't much hope and his heart went out to the man whose only concern was the love of his life. Tears rolled down his face as he cried out her name over and over—Harper!

Mr. Weaver's sleep was fitful and he awoke to find Mrs. Weaver standing over him, suitcase in one hand, a ticket for Jamaica in the other.

She held up a white-gloved hand. "I've got a one-way ticket to paradise."

He shot out of bed. "Don't you think we should talk this over?"

"I have."

"Not with me." He pulled on a pair of pants.

"Raoul says he loves me." She fanned her neck.

"I—love you—and you're my wife!" Mr. Weaver reminded her; forgetting to ask, *Who's Raoul?*

"It's not the same." She sat on the edge of their bed and sighed. "You're like an overripe banana whose time is done: mawkish, mushy, and you have brown spots." She pointed to his hands. Her voice was empty and dull, like an old kitchen knife, and it gleaned flesh from bone in ragged swipes.

She looked at Mr. Weaver and a shiver of revulsion rippled through her torso. He flinched when he saw it. He wanted to yell: *Get used to that feeling, you strumpet. That's me dancing on your grave.* But snappy comebacks would elude him for weeks. In the moment, he was speechless; even dumbfounded.

"I can tell you're going to be nasty in our trial separation. Raoul warned me; told me I may as well head straight for a divorce!" She rose from the bed and collected her suitcase. She opened Mr. Weaver's closet and removed a cream-coloured Panama hat.

"I'm taking this." She placed the hat in a carry-on bag.

"But it's mine." Mr. Weaver had been diminished to a man who argued over an ugly hat. He wanted to scream in her ear that a good man, a decent man, had died that evening, while Mr. Weaver held his hand. The very last thing he expected to learn about that night was his wife's lover and her one-way ticket to paradise.

She shrugged. "Raoul needs one. But since you're so attached . . ." She threw the hat at him. "Keep it."

Mrs. Weaver pulled back the bedroom curtains and looked outside. "Taxi's here."

Mr. Weaver crawled back into bed.

"You probably know this, but . . ." She pulled the covers off his head. "Listen up, mister, this is important. That girl Debbie knows, Harper Steele something-or-other: the one who had a kid in high school. You know the one I mean—Debbie sold her Cynthia's old baby stuff—" She paused as she put the final items in her handbag. "I wonder if she ever got paid?"

"Anyhow, Debbie told me the guy Harper's shacked up with died in a car crash tonight—Debbie figures he was drunk. So tomorrow I want you to give Debbie an update. Debbie's Bill is looking for work and this guy's job is *available*." Mrs. Weaver drew quotation marks in the air. "Early bird, fat worms, and all that."

"The man was her husband." Mr. Weaver pulled himself to a sitting position, holding his head in his hands.

"If that's what the girl wants to call him. Po/ta/to, po/tat/o. It's all the same to me."

He twisted the wedding ring from his finger, walked to the toilet, and flushed. "Leave your keys, lock the door, and get out."

"Well! That's a fine goodbye after thirty-five years of marriage." She stomped down the stairs to the sounds of a sullied wedding band clinking and clanging its way through the sewer pipes. Mrs. Weaver threw the keys on the floor. "Lock your own stupid door!"

She said she'd write, but she never did. A week later the bank called to say she overdrew Mr. Weaver's account; he could kiss his new boat goodbye. A month later, Mrs. Weaver's lawyer wrote to start divorce proceedings—apparently, paradise was expensive.

The following morning his heart skipped a beat. Things would never be the same. How could they? That was three years ago, and now, here he was, doing the unthinkable. He'd slept in, again.

****

Mr. Weaver dressed, hopped on his bicycle and pedalled over to Harper's. It was no surprise to find a police car parked by the curb. He rapped on the screen door. "Harper?"

Truebell answered. "Where's your mother, son? I need to speak with her." Mr. Weaver pushed past and hurried into the kitchen. It was worse than he'd feared—the cop had her in cuffs. "Stop! She didn't do it!" Harper and Finn looked up as Mr. Weaver charged through the doorway.

"It's okay; he's just showing me how they work." Harper lifted her arm and slipped the cuffs off her wrist. "See?"

"I'll see a lot better with a cup of coffee in me." Mr. Weaver admitted to Harper. "Black." He glowered at the detective. "*If* you have any left."

Harper poured him a fresh cup of Columbian Dark Roast. It was his favourite and one of the many reasons he was so fond of her, although that wasn't true—anything she offered him was his favourite. Mr. Weaver thanked Harper and squeezed between her and the detective.

"Razor not working this morning?" She gave his face an affectionate rub.

"I slept in."

Harper looked surprised.

"It happens—mostly to other people—but today it was my turn. Again."

"You look like a grizzly bear." Sydney observed over her morning bowl of fruit sprinkled with granola. "I like it."

Mr. Weaver thanked Sydney and then asked if he could speak to Harper in private. "Away from little ears?" She nodded and they stepped outside.

"What's this about, Dallas?" She used his first name. He liked it. He couldn't remember the last time a woman had called him by his given name. Her voice fell like spring rain on his parched soul.

"I came about Miss Newman . . ." He hesitated to say more with the detective hovering so close.

"It's okay, Dallas . . ." Finn caught the indignant glare. "Pardon me, *Mr. Weaver*. We released her early this morning—on her own recognizance."

"Miss Newman is asleep upstairs." Harper tilted her head toward the second-floor windows.

". . . under *your* roof?!"

"Yes." She laughed.

When True could restrain himself no longer, he picked up Sydney and carried her outside. "I was just as shocked as you, Mr. Weaver, when mom asked Ben and me to make up the spare room."

"I'll bet." Mr. Weaver shoved his hands into his pockets and pursed his lips. He could feel the wheels turning in Harper's mind, *Why, Dallas. What an odd thing to say*. He shifted gears and waded back in with a question.

"So, detective, what about the b-o-d-y?" (He spelled out the word.) "The one you guys pulled off her front lawn?"

Finn was still getting used to small communities where gossip travelled like wildfire. He raised an eyebrow. "Why? What have you heard?" The boys tittered as did Harper.

"What's so funny, Mommy?"

"Exactly my thoughts, young lady." Finn flipped open his notebook.

"It's nothing *vile*." Harper struggled to explain.

"Or, noteworthy." Dallas chimed in, trying to wrangle his neighbourhood recon work into something benevolent. "I'm just your friendly eye in the sky—that's all." He puffed out his chest.

Finn waited, notebook in hand.

"Harmless   .   .   ." Dallas knew   he   was   losing ground. He dropped his shoulders.

"And where's the location of this *eye in the sky*, as you call it?"

Sydney flashed Finn a big smile and raised her hand to answer. "He's the birdman! Up in the tree!" She pointed to the massive maple visible from Harper's patio—an entire two blocks, one alley, and three yards over.

"She is a beauty." Dallas conceded.

The antics of Sydney's birdman were never a secret, at least not a well-kept one. Everyone was in on the joke, everyone except Miss Newman who listened with interest from the window of Harper's guest bedroom.

CHAPTER TEN

Terri stepped back from the window and rested on the edge of the bed; she was spent. When she was detained by the police, she envisioned nothing but defeat; her tank was empty and her long-time tormentor was revved up on crazy juice. But the morning gave way to a new perspective. It was time for *him* to vanish. She picked up her cell.

"Margaret? I think he's found me."

"Hang on, Terri." She pressed mute and directed her staff to leave the room. "Tell me everything, but first, are you okay?"

Terri took several slow breaths and relayed the events of the past twenty-four hours: the candy, the iced tea, the boys, the cat, and the cuffs. She ended with Harper taking her in and giving her safe harbour. "All things being equal? Better than expected."

Margaret Lamb, attorney at law, private investigator, and mostly, long-time family friend, leaned back in her chair. As she waited for Terri to continue, she watched the choreographed precision of the window washer as he cleaned the city grime from her windows; suspended thirty-seven floors above the ground. She suddenly envied his freedom and wanted to pry open the large window pane and join him.

"What do you want to do?"

How had such a simple question become so loaded? Since the passing of Terri's parents, Margaret hadn't kept in touch. But she remembered firsthand the toll this case had taken on the family. *What to do, indeed?* Terri's parents had asked Margaret the same question many times. While she was duty-bound to uphold the law, let's just say their solution for the recruit was far and away outside that realm and much more "final."

"Let's finish him—it. I mean *it.*" She didn't mean *it*, but that was the correct thing to say to a lawyer.

Margaret understood. She wanted this to be over as well. How many times had Terri called her in the middle of the night, breathless, fearful that he was outside her door? More times than she could count. It was time to finish him—*it*.

A lifetime ago, Terri had worked at 15 Wing Moose Jaw as a firefighter. Most people overlooked this, but there was a time when her strapping figure turned more than a few heads—and not in a curious, "circusy" fashion. She was pretty in her own right, balmy in her own morbid way, and strong in—well—in everyone's way.

Terri also volunteered with the city's local fire department where a certain recruit took a fancy to her. But she was a career gal, and he wanted a doting do-nothing wife. She liked her men seasoned: tall, lean, crispy around the edges, and cooked to tender perfection. In other words: bacon. Terri compared the recruit to an egg: scrambled.

One time she lied and told him she preferred women, but that only intensified his interest; sending him on a mission to get her batting for the *right* team. For months he assaulted her with gifts: industrial grade steel toe boots, moleskin lined gloves, flimsy lingerie, and a flannel onesie covered in pink hearts, bunnies, and unicorns. Still, she was unmoved. According to him, Terri had barricaded the door to her heart, and only *his* extraordinary love could crack it open.

Then he noticed Terri sporting a stylish lavender scarf around her neck. He confronted her because it could only mean one thing: she was double-timing him. Terri tried to explain: if she had never one-timed him, how could she be guilty of two-timing him? He chose to ignore this logic and decided to curse her and the day she was born.

She naively believed this had ended his obsession—until stuffed taxidermy animals showed up at the base wearing scarves tied in hangman knots. Terri reported it to the company commander. When they appeared on the steps outside her home, she reported it to the local police. And when she found a beheaded mannequin straddled across the hood of her car, she disappeared.

That was fifteen years ago.

"He's stepped up his game, Terri."

"Where do you suppose he got the body?"

Margaret hesitated, not anxious to sink into the sludge he called a mind. She stuck a toe into his grey matter and tested the *water*. He wasn't clever, but he was laser focused and still looking to redress Terri's crime of not wanting him, these fifteen years later. If this was him, he wouldn't be satisfied until Terri came crawling back on her hands and knees, begging for forgiveness.

"On some level he wants you dead, but he's too much of a coward to pull the trigger."

The phone slipped from Terri's hand.

"Terri—? Talk to me—please. You can do this. I know you can. Let's start by making a list of all the things we know about him—"

"I know he's a . . ." she rambled off a long list of expletives.

Margaret laughed. "Now tell me something I don't know. Tell me about his family, friends, work, hobbies. That sort of thing."

Terri centered herself and set the charges to blow the doors from her encrusted memory banks, but they were reinforced—they put up a fight. It was a survival tactic, and deep down she feared opening that spigot. At first just a trickle came: his occupation, his passion for tinkering with engines. Then the sensory memories surfaced: the feelings he evoked; the smell of his skin—sweaty, salty, and acrid; the sound of his voice—country twang with a bit of southern charm. It all came flooding back.

"I don't recall that he had many friends. His stepfather is, or was, a wealthy funeral home owner in Moose Jaw; he's the one who made sure I lost the court case. He made everything go away—even me."

"Okay, let's start there. Let's apply Occam's razor," Margaret said. "Funeral homes have bodies. Is it possible he still has contact with, or access to the funeral home?"

Terri straightened and wiped her nose. "I'd wager he stole the body."

"Possibly." Margaret frowned. "But if that's true, why haven't any family members come forward? It hasn't made the news and a missing body is a big deal. Or, at least, it should be."

"What if the man was homeless?"

The litigator in Margaret only looked for hard facts, ones she could use to make a case stick. "I don't think we should jump to conclusions."

Terri's shoulders sagged. "Do you think it's possible—that he killed somebody?"

"It's possible, but for now let's just say he stole a body."

Margaret explained that an unclaimed body was kept chilled—ready to go—and it seemed possible that no one would miss it for days, maybe weeks. Then all the recruit had to do was transport the body to Terri's house and dump it on her doorstep. It was almost too easy.

"But you're talking premeditation, Margaret. I'm not sure he's that capable."

"It may surprise you to learn how obsessing for fifteen years changes a person."

"No, that much I understand."

Terri placed her faith in Margaret; she was a constant friend in this storm, but her mind couldn't let go of one sticky detail—

"How did he find me?"

"I'm Googling Rundle's Landing as we speak. For all we know he's an internet junkie with nothing better to do than search for you."

"For all I know he's been playing cat and mouse with me for fifteen years; hiding in the wings, waiting for the perfect moment to pounce, waiting for me to let down my guard. And I did, Margaret. I got sloppy when I moved here. And now this? A man is found dead on my front lawn. What was I thinking? Believing I could have a sane life." Terri hung up and lay back on the bed.

****

To this day, Terri simply referred to him as the recruit. She wouldn't allow him the dignity of a name. But the Moose Jaw Herald Times saw things differently. They blasted out his name, his picture, and the list of his charges: harassment, public mischief, and stalking.

Rand Jared Ng was the stepson of a prominent businessman who had no intention of seeing his business ridiculed by the antics of his second wife's *scrambled egg* son. He dumped truckloads of cash into his stepson's defense and it worked. By the time the verdict was read aloud in court, dismissed on all counts with prejudice, Terri was long gone.

****

For more than a decade she kept a low profile, changing from firefighter to 9-1-1 dispatch. It kept her involved in the work she loved, but at a safe, arms-length distance that didn't draw much attention. Her life became small and for that she resented Ng, not to mention the legal system. When the opportunity presented itself to work for Rundle's Landing Emergency Dispatch office, she jumped with both feet and landed with a small tidal wave. She was done being small.

Three months later, Terri permanently relocated. The transition was a slow process—it had to be perfect. She had to be sure. And she was—to the point of interacting with others, for no other reason other than it made her smile. And this was her weakness; not that she would change one terrible thing that happened. Not for the world.

Terri's usual habit when working was to make time for a stroll around Rundle's Pond. As soon as her feet touched the walkway, she synced with the natural rhythm of the park. She loved the earthly scent of vegetation; the crisp, crackling sounds made when someone across a bed of leaves, and the richness of the fall colours: reds, yellows, purples, and the stubborn green leaves—refusing to declare summer was at an end. But it was the water that called her by name.

Rundle's Pond was broad and plump, like a nice rump roast for Sunday dinner. In some spots, you could plumb her depth to forty-five feet, and she was lined with sharp, sloping edges along her banks. She was enchanting to look at, but not a pond to challenge. Ice crossings in winter were perilous and no matter the number of signs posted or the words of warning shouted, someone always thought they were smarter, quicker, and lighter than air. The pond always won: claiming heavy parkas, backpacks and winter boots until the following spring.

After a heavy rain, she often swelled beyond her banks, leaving hundreds of coy fish stranded in muddy puddles along the walkway. These were relatives of the fish little Jimmy Harlow had released a good ten years earlier. Somehow, they'd survived despite the frigid winters, thick ice pack, and the pelicans that scooped them up like front-end loaders at a buffet.

On one of Terri's walks, she had circled the pond for the second time when she noticed a small bit of clothing floating near the far shore. She could see a group of boys playing flag football, but no parents or other children close to the water's edge. She massaged the skin on her forearms and felt the tiny hairs prickle against her cotton sleeves. Then she saw it, a creamy-looking doll's hand bobbing between the cattails.

"Oh, my Lord, there's a child in the water!"

She waved her arms, desperate to capture someone's attention, but the boisterous football players were too caught up in their game to notice her. She charged down the grassy bank shrieking, "Call 9-1-1!" A young couple close by continued to play Frisbee, two moms drank their pumpkin spice lattes and chatted while their children played on the swings. Terri tried them all, but no one answered. She knew she had to swim for it.

She kicked off her shoes, dropped her purse and jacket, and lunged into the soupy green liquid. She skimmed across the top of the water, beating back lily pads, clumps of twigs, and withering leaves. When she reached the other side, she lowered her legs to stand. Mud crept over her feet, penetrating her nylon stockings and cementing her to the bottom. Powered by an extreme adrenalin rush, she plunged her arms deep into the water, frantic to find the child's body—praying she wasn't too late.

People around the lake started to take notice. Some laughed at the sight of this strange woman splashing in the water until one boy from the football game began to wail. It sent a chill down everyone's spine. He screamed out a name.

"SYDNEY!!!!"

Terri continued to rake the water until she felt the brush of little fingers on her arm. She pulled the child free of the miry depths with all of her strength. A little girl flew into the air, landing in the arms of the woman who had just pulled her from a certain watery grave.

"Sydney!"

The boy flung himself into the water and ripped the limp body from Terri. He carried her onto the shore just as the sirens from the ambulance approached. There was mass confusion. People jockeyed for position to get a look at the blue child, and the boy who had rescued her.

No one seemed to notice the drenched woman with lily pads and twigs stuck to her clothing, standing a mere three meters off shore. She was holding a small orange shoe in her hand as she waded ashore. Terri placed it on the grass and drunkenly walked back to her coat and purse. The young Asian couple who'd been playing Frisbee headed toward the ambulance and police. Shaken, they recounted their story to a reporter and posed for a photo.

Terri spotted her belongings lying in the same scattered piles she'd left them. She took a moment to languish on the grass and catch her breath. The drone of the sirens pounded in her brain. She tugged off her stockings and used them to wipe the mud from her feet. When her shoes refused to slip on, she plodded barefoot down the trail to the parking lot. She was a soggy, squelching woman carrying shoes and a jacket, her purse slung loosely over one shoulder, and reeking like a wet pooch.

The following day, the Rundle's Landing Gazette reported that due to the quick thinking of a new immigrant family, a little girl's life had been spared; she was rescued by her brother, Truebell.

CHAPTER ELEVEN

"Thanks for the coffee, Harper." Finn set his cup in the sink as he took his leave. "I believe I've got all the details, but if there's anything else that needs clearing up, I'll give you a call."

"Anytime." She smiled up at him.

Finn leaned in and motioned with his hand. "There's something on your teeth—"

Harper gasped. She spun around and scowled at the boys. She pretended to cough.

"Thanks for nothing."

"It was the least we could do, Mom."

Ben snorted. "Nice smile, Mrs. Salmon."

"Dishes! Now!"

****

Terri listened for the house to quiet down and then stepped from the guest bedroom into the hallway. Harper had lined it with family photos: herself, Truebell, Sydney, and a man with kind eyes. Terri felt certain he must be the children's father. She lingered by his frame.

"That was my dad." Truebell loomed behind her.

Terri looked from True to the picture of his handsome father. She recognized the eyes and the dimple on the left cheek. "I see the resemblance." She smiled.

She held out her hand. "I don't think we've met."

"I know who you are—" He turned on his heels and banged down the stairs to the kitchen.

"Mom! Miss Newman's awake." He belched into the house.

Terri paused and nodded to Mr. Salmon's image. "Ah, there's the difference. Good luck with that boy." She brushed a speck of dust from his photo and proceeded down the staircase.

"Good morning, Miss Newman." Harper was brilliant; she was Venus rising. "Will you join us for breakfast?"

"No, but thank you. I have urgent business at home." She gathered up her purse and removed her house key.

"Well, you are more than welcome to join my family and me anytime you like." Harper buzzed; always making honey, seldom taking any.

Terri shifted her gaze toward the odd-looking creature intently gaping at her. "Oh, dear, where are my manners? Miss Newman, please meet my friend and neighbour, Mr. Weaver."

The 6'2" lanky frame rose from the chair and presented a calloused hand. "My pleasure, Miss Newman."

Hmm, she thought, *it speaks*. Terri liked his looks, but there was no reason to lose her head over his lodgepole pine exterior. "Are you the man who lives in a tree and spies on people?"

"I wouldn't call it spying, per se, and I don't *live* in a tree," he squeaked.

Terri regarded this stranger with cool detachment. She decided to lay an axe to this timber and watch it fall.

"And what interesting things have you learned about me, Mr. Weaver?"

He mumbled something incomprehensible, placed his empty cup in the sink, and made for the door before she could stab him to death with her icy stare. His reddening face convicted him as he thrust his way through the door and stomped down the steps. Sitting astride his bicycle he glanced back at the house and the silhouette of Miss Newman against the screen door.

Harper was at a loss. This was not how she saw their introduction playing out.

"Has Mr. Weaver offended you?"

"Yes, dear Harper, I believe he has violated the privacy of my home and my liberty. Without those things, I have nothing. Do you understand?"

Harper shrugged. "I'm not sure."

Terri sighed. "I hope you never need to." She thanked Harper again and made her way home.

CHAPTER TWELVE

Simpson perked up as Finn entered the squad room. "So, hey, what'd you think?"

"She's not your type."

"Yeah, well, you can't fault a fellow for trying . . ." Sonny smoothed his tie and adjusted the diamond clip.

Finn slammed shut an open drawer on his desk. The office mice had been busy while he was away—they'd left him two crayons from the movie "UP," a chewed-off pencil, and a package of pine nuts. *Nice touch.*

"What have we learned about our vic?"

Simpson whistled through his teeth. "Okay, back to business." He rolled his chair over to Finn's desk. "This is what we know." He held up the tattered piece of newsprint found at the scene.

"Hey, Verna?" Finn pointed to the newsprint. "Can you make a photocopy of this? It's getting pretty dog-eared."

"Both sides?"

"What's that?"

"I asked if you wanted both sides photocopied," said Verna. Finn walked over to the copier and flipped the page. She patted his arm, grabbed her coffee, and headed outside for a smoke. "You realize, hon, it'd be a lot faster if you did this yourself."

"Yeah, sorry," he called after her.

"Sonny? Did you see this?" He held up the reverse side of the page. It was a picture taken at Rundle's Pond with a smiling young couple standing by the shore. The caption read: **Rundle's Newest Family Saves One of Its Own.**

"Who'd they save?"

Sonny typed in a few key strokes. "Her name is Sydney Ella Salmon. Isn't that Harper's kid?"

"Huh? There's a shoe in the picture. I wonder what colour is it?"

". . . and what size?" said Sonny.

"Let's find out. This is too much of a coincidence."

****

The kid at the Gazette couldn't find anything they asked for.

"It's a photo from a couple of months back: Asian couple, new to town, little girl almost drowned, Rundle's Pond. Any of that seem familiar?" Finn thumped his fingers on the countertop.

"Perhaps you've got it stored somewhere . . . digitally?" Sonny suggested.

"Nope, not that one."

"Why not?" Both men asked at once.

"Because it's a contract piece," he told them. "See? The byline gives his name: Rand Jared Ng. He doesn't work here. The paper paid him $25 for a hard copy of the picture."

"Isn't that unusual?" Finn pressed the kid.

"Yup. Sounds like someone who surfs the web for images, prints them off and claims them as his own."

"That sounds unethical."

"It's $25 bucks. Who cares?"

"Spoken like a true capitalist."

"Hey, man, it's not like we have time to be scouring Facebook and Instagram for every slice of the gossip pie."

Finn grabbed the kid by his collar. "Drownings are not gossip. Got it?"

"Got it, dude. But you don't need to grab me with your nostrils all flared and stuff."

Sonny took Finn by the arm. "Let's get out of here before *you* turn into a headline."

Finn sunk into the passenger seat of the car. "What aren't we seeing?"

"In the first place, I'm not seeing lunch." Sonny poked himself in the gut. "And in the second place, I can't understand anything until I eat lunch. After that, I'll pull the reports from the incident and compare them to the newspaper story. Agreed?"

CHAPTER THIRTEEN

Mr. Weaver was still chafed over his exchange with Miss Newman. He wished he could put a finger on the exact cause of the feelings burrowing beneath his skin. It was a familiar feeling, but at the same time it felt foreign. When he could stand it no longer, he pedalled off to confront her.

He coasted downhill to her house and found her sitting on the front steps, sorting through a debris field. In the soft afternoon light, she no longer raised his ire.

He leaned his bicycle against her veranda. "May I help?"

"Oh, Mr. Weaver." Terri tossed the shattered pieces of glass she'd gathered into a bucket and removed her gloves. "I'm glad you came. I was too hard on you back at Harper's, and I owe you an apology."

"No, you were right. I infringe on people's lives." He took off his cap and held it in his hands. "I'm Peter Pan, waiting for someone to open the window."

His honesty moved her—*the old lodgepole pine had more guts than met the eye*. "I'll be honest, I was afraid you had a hand in this." She motioned to her front lawn. "I see now I was mistaken."

"One man did all this?"

"Two little mice helped things along—"

"Then that settles it, Miss Newman, you're not safe here. Grab an overnight bag. You're staying with me."

She lifted a palm and put the kibosh on his enthusiasm. "I can plainly see I'm not the type of woman you're used to being with,

48

Mr. Weaver." His cheeks burned hot, not even the sweat dripping from his forehead could douse the flames. "Let's get one thing straight. I never stay with someone when we're not on a first-name basis." She gave him a *gotcha look* and winked.

He exhaled. "It's Dallas."

"Nice to meet you, Dallas. And, may I add, not through the end of your night vision goggles."

His ruddy face glowed once more.

"You never suspected that I knew?" She shook her head— *men*. "You really should invest in a pair of non-reflective lenses . . ."

"How about we catch up on those details later."

There was that itch again. She'd snared him and he liked it. Dallas sensed she was his kryptonite; his knees trembled. He narrowed his eyes and put on his cap. "For now, I'd like to get home before nightfall."

"I'm good with that. Let me get my bag." She stepped into the house and retrieved a small overnight tote.

When she came out, she glanced at his bicycle and asked if that was the getaway vehicle. He could find no words to reassure her, to tell her everything would be okay. Instead, he held her hand.

"Leave your car. Maybe we can fool him into believing you're at home."

"Or, maybe he's watching us right this minute and laughing over how easy it'll be the next time." Dallas gritted his teeth.

As evening fell, they hiked up the hill to his home. Dallas pushed his bike and carried her tote. If he were a younger man, he would have slung Terri over one shoulder—fireman style. He sized up her bottom.

"Don't even think about it, old man!"

CHAPTER FOURTEEN

It was nearing 4:00 p.m. when Margaret Lamb placed a call to Rundle PD, Detective Yung's desk.

"You know, Ms. Lamb, your concern for Miss Newman's safety is admirable, but if you're acting as her legal counsel, I need a name. And if you're calling as her friend, I still need a name."

"The court dismissed his charges, with prejudice. I can't."

"Well, tell me this much, does the name Rand Jared Ng mean anything to you?"

She held her breath. "I've never met anyone by that name. Why?"

"It's probably nothing. The guy sent in a picture of a near drowning that took place at Rundle's Pond a few months back."

"Rundle's Pond? That's interesting."

"How so?" Finn shifted the phone to his other ear.

"—just thinking out loud; wondering what the connection might be."

"Us, too." He breathed into the phone. "Listen, it's been a long day and if there's nothing else you can offer . . .?"

Margaret had nothing else—for him. She hung up and placed a second call.

****

Simpson walked over to Finn's desk and tossed the full-length printed story of the near drowning on his desk.

"What am I looking for?" Finn was feeling cross-eyed with all the research.

"Skip down to the second-to-the-last paragraph—a detail that the paper felt was outside the immediate story, so they buried it. It looks like no one else caught it."

"No one except this Ng fella." Finn read the article out loud.

A young Asian couple who had been picnicking at Rundle's Pond told this reporter that a crazy woman charged toward them. She waved her arms in the air and demanded they call 9-1-1. They were so frightened that they did exactly that. It wasn't until later they realized a child had entered the water and was being rescued on the far side of the pond. They told police they were in fear for their lives and ran away from the woman. No one else reported seeing her.

On the other side of the pond, little Sydney's brother, Truebell, dove into the water and saved her. It's being touted as a miracle by all who witnessed this dramatic event.

"How'd we miss the part about the woman?"

"Let's compare it to the police report."

Sonny cross-referenced every detail of the two stories. "Checks out." He threw his pen across the desk.

"Not so fast." Finn straightened. "How did the brother know where to find his sister? People reported him running in circles and screaming her name from the middle of the playing field."

"He wasn't paying attention, he was *playing football.*" Simpson held up the sworn witness testimonies.

"Call Mrs. Salmon. She needs to bring in her son." Finn slumped down in his chair. Some days he hated being good at his job.

****

Harper was in the midst of preparing dinner when the call came. She hung up and immediately yelled, "Truebell!"

She buckled Sydney into her car seat and the three of them made the silent ride to the police station. Harper shuddered recalling a similar trip she'd made three years earlier. She remembered that the wipers could scarcely keep up to the rain and the left one kept sticking, smearing greasy insect guts across the windshield. It was a fearful, searing memory that would not wash away.

"It's just a fender bender," Harper told her parents when she dropped off the children. Truebell searched his mother's stoic face for a hint of comfort, a glimmer of hope. She kissed them both and ran back to the car. As she pulled away from the curb, Harper focused on the beam of light thrown by her headlights. She refused to address the boy standing at the front door, holding his baby sister as the rain poured down without mercy.

****

The ICU monitors beeped and whirred as Harper hurried down the polished hallway, but when she entered his room Reggie caught sight of her and the beeping went wild: 60, 120, 240 beats per minute. After that, staff wouldn't allow her see him, or him to see her—it was a double-edged sword that cut both ways.

"We're doing our best to keep him calm, Mrs. Salmon." The doctor stressed the seriousness of the situation upon her. "He's lost a great deal of blood."

"But he's my husband. He needs me," she wailed and collapsed to the floor "Please, I need him."

Moments later the beeping turned to a monotonous hum. Harper covered her ears.

"Turn it off," the doctor said. "I'm calling it."

Harper continued to lie on the cold linoleum. As she did, an image flashed through her brain, *like mother, like son,* and she took up her post, guarding his door. After staff had disconnected the tubes and wires from her husband's body, and they'd retreated to give her space, she entered the room and closed the door.

She filled a plastic basin with warm water and collected a stack of fresh towels and soap. Harper brushed the hair from his forehead, still sticky with crimson blood, and kissed his cool lips. "Well, my love, let's get you freshened up."

Harper put her hand to her chest as she drove toward the police station. It still hurt to remember, to need him, and worst of all, to relive letting him go.

****

She pulled into the Visitors parking and marched inside with her son. Finn greeted the Salmon family at the door. "Oh? You brought Sydney." He gave Harper an awkward smile. "Would it be okay if Verna watched her for a few minutes while we talk?"

Verna nodded. Sydney perused the stash of mermaids on her desk and decided it would be okay with her, too.

"We won't be long, love bug."

"Take your time, Harper. I got some playing to do."

Sonny was already in the conference room when they entered. He introduced himself to Harper and Truebell. Finn pulled out two reports and slapped them in front of True. "A tough day, I'm sure," he said.

"Uh huh." True glanced at the paper. All he could see was a torrent of words circling on the page, Sydney drowning, and him being swept away.

"Want to tell us about it?" Sonny pulled his chair beside True.

"Tell you what?" Harper crossed her legs and then folded her arms across her chest.

"It's best if he speaks for himself," said Finn.

"Which part?" True pushed his hair to one side and tried to focus on the words facing him.

"The part you left out about Miss Newman."

"Or, the part you left out about playing touch football and forgetting to watch your little sister." Sonny tossed this into the mix to see if it would float.

Harper swept the pages aside. Her voice was electrifying, filled with crackles and high voltage. "What?!"

"It's not my fault! I set her down on the blanket and told her to stay."

"Your sister isn't a . . . puppy." Harper's brain couldn't make sense of what she'd just heard. The pain in her chest exploded.

"And then what happened?" Finn bumped his chair into True's.

"And then there was a bunch of commotion by the water and some woman was making a big show of shoving her hands in and out of the water. We all thought she was crazy. We laughed. Okay?" Harper issued a loud cry and covered her mouth, willing the pain to stop. It didn't. It couldn't.

"The next thing I knew she was holding Sydney in her arms. She was blue and she wasn't breathing . . ." Tears streamed down his face. "I ran as fast as I could and grabbed her."

"*From Miss Newman?*" Finn held up True's statement—the one where he'd lied.

"Yes." His answer was barely audible. "But then she showed up, again, living right behind us; and sleeping in our guest bedroom. I panicked."

"What do you mean you *panicked?*" Harper glared at her son.

"What does that mean, Truebell?" The hurt and the pain were churning. She roiled.

"Last night, Ben and I snuck a bottle of rum from the liquor cabinet. After a few drinks we went back to Miss Newman's . . ."

"Went back?" It was a chorus of three.

"We were the ones who stole her candy."

Harper spun his chair to face her. At that moment, he wanted to be anywhere but in her crosshairs. "You're admitting that once was not enough? That you had to go back and inflict more pain on the woman who saved your sister's life because you were playing football!"

Verna caught Finn's attention and gave him a pained expression. She motioned for them to lower the volume while she and Sydney played in the outer part of the office.

"You need water, Harper. Drink." Finn thrust a bottle into her hands. It was an order, not a suggestion.

"Yes, I do." Harper paced around the room, tempted to give her son a firm knuckle-rub each time she passed him.

"Go on, Truebell. What happened next?" Sonny's voice was reassuring, it said: *Trust me, kid. I'm your friend.* Harper wanted to reassure him with her foot. She sat back down and took a swig of water.

"It was a threat, I guess. I didn't stop to think it through." He ran his hands through his hair and pulled on it. For the first time he looked at his mom, bottled water dripping from her chin. "I wanted things to go back; be like they were with Dad. I wanted you to look at me the way you used to: like your son, and not some loser."

"Truebell! Tell us right now what you and Ben did to Miss Newman?" It was Finn's turn. His tone was much more compelling. Harper flinched with fear for her son and his future.

"We threw that old shoe of Sydney's on the lawn—the orange one from the hospital. I guess the other shoe is still suctioned to the bottom of the pond. Then we tossed a copy of the Gazette story on her front porch and broke the rum bottle over the Crypt Keeper's head. We stabbed him with it, too. That's when we discovered he was real. Real dead, that is. I knew it earlier, but Ben insisted he was wet from the sprinklers. He wasn't."

"So, you stayed and spoke to the police like the responsible young men you are?"

He threw an exasperated look in Sonny's direction. "You know that isn't true! We ran home and hid in the tent like two five-year-old's. That's when Mom showed up and told us to get inside."

Finn took a deep breath. "Okay, this is good. We're making progress. Now, what time did you first see the body . . . the Crypt Keeper?"

"I forget." He looked at his mom. "What time was curfew last night?"

"It was 10—like always—like forever!" Harper railed while she beat out every syllable with her fist.

"Okay, I remember now. It was 9:53. I remember because I had seven minutes to get home after the ransacking."

"And you kiss your mom and sister with those same lips?" Sonny rubbed his mouth with the back of his hand.

"Sometimes . . ." True kept his eyes on the floor.

Harper grabbed her son and pushed aside a tussle of hair. She held his face in her hands. She'd not been this close in months—maybe years. Here was her young son, the one who was still standing guard at her parents' front door, waiting for normal to return.

"I'll leave home if you want me to."

Harper floundered at the prospect of losing another member of her family.

"Just like Dad," he said.

She gathered her strength, picked up the water bottle and dumped the contents over his head. "Your place is with me! Me! Not with your father." She threw the empty bottle at the recycle bin. "Got it?" She'd always wondered how it felt to love someone and hate them at the same time. Now she understood.

"I loved your father, but he's gone and I can't bring him back and just the thought of that fills me with rage. I get so angry I could . . ." She grabbed his arm and pinched it. "*You* are staying here with *me* until I say otherwise. And don't even think about trying to live with Grandma and Grandpa, or Ben." She shook her finger at him and her face softened. "Are we clear?"

He nodded and wiped his eyes.

"I don't want to hurt you, True, but if you ever do something like this again . . ." She ran through a list of possible sentences for him. "I'll . . ." She looked at his head. "I'll shave off all your hair and you can kiss any chance with Cynthia Dowd goodbye. You can tell her, *Adios amiga!*"

He peeked out from beneath his hair. "You know about Cynthia?"

Harper groaned and swung her attention to Finn. "Are you charging my son with anything?"

"No, Miss Newman wouldn't hear of it."

Sonny crept in with his twinkling blue eyes. "We never really thought he was the killer." Harper stared at him.

"Just trying to lighten the mood . . ." Sonny sucked in his lips and adjusted his tie.

"Take your son home." Finn held the door for her and waited for it to shut tight.

"What's the matter with you, Sonny?!"

"What? I thought it went pretty well." Sonny peacocked around the room. He stood in profile before his reflection in the two-way glass and tightened his abs. "I think she fancied me; a real man's man."

"Back to business, Casanova, the clock's ticking." Finn left the conference room and tapped his keyboard.

Sonny followed him to his desk "Okay, here's a shot in the dark. Who do we know with surveillance equipment in the Opal Meadows subdivision?"

Finn walked over to the window that overlooked the parking lot. Another day had faded away. And with it, another missed opportunity to get outside and enjoy the fall weather; maybe kick up leaves before the trees were naked, their branches laid bare—

He ran back to his desk and punched Sonny in the arm. "Sometimes I like the way you think, Simpson." Sonny beamed and scanned the room to see who else had caught the compliment.

"Verna?" Finn sang out. She sighed, sat back down, and stowed her handbag in the desk drawer.

"One more favour before you go home . . .?" His voice softened and melted any resolve she'd had of refusing seconds earlier. Thoughts of getting home on time, or to the aroma wafting from her crock pot vanished. Her saucy BBQ meatballs would have to keep. She hoisted her droopy pantyhose and replaced her purple high-tops with a classic pair of Tender Tootsie strappy sandals.

"Ready." She cracked her knuckles; her magic fingers hovered over the keyboard. "Let's have it."

CHAPTER FIFTEEN

"Mom, when we get home I'm going straight over to Miss Newman's and apologize."

Harper rubbed his head. "You're a good kid. Why not ask her if she wants to sleep over again? Or, have a late supper with us?"

He nodded.

She eased the car into Rosewood cul-de-sac and rolled to a stop in front of their house. While she unbuckled Sydney, True skirted around back and through the gate to Miss Newman's. He could see her car in the driveway, but the house lights were off.

"Maybe she's having a nap?" It reminded him of his grandparents who were in bed by 8:30 every night. *Must be an old people thing*, he mused.

"Or, maybe she's having a dirt nap . . ." a male voice quipped.

True's skin crawled from his collar bones to the top of his shoulders in waves. The man's voice was pungent and it froze him in place beneath the shadow of a big spruce—home to the dozen or more bats just stirring from their roosts.

"Come on out, kid. I know you're shakin' in your little short pants."

The man lit a cigarette and inhaled, his lungs billowing puffs of smoke signals up and away from the veranda. "Come on, boy. Come have a smoke with me. I don't bite—at least not like your little sister." He let his words tumble like someone rummaging through a pile of dirty laundry, looking for a fresh pair of underwear—all the while knowing none would be found.

"Well, kid, let's put it this way . . . either you come out or I'll pay your sexy mom and your cutie pie little sister a visit." He sniffed the air. "I think she's making me supper!"

Truebell stepped into the clearing.

"Aw ... what a handsome boy! But, you're taller than I last remember."

Truebell inspected him. He was ordinary, even plain, with a next-door-neighbour, serial-killer casualness about him. "Did you kill that man?"

"Me?! You've been trolling in the wrong catnip, young fella. Terri Newman crushed the life out of that beast." He cocked his ear. "What? Surprised?"

He took another drag. "Yup, 'tis true. Or, should I say, 'tis true, True." He spit out a few strands of tobacco. "I know everything about you and your stinking little family. I know what you and your buddy Ben did in the *shadows*, and I know what your momma wishes she could do. Maybe I could help her with that . . . What do you think—*son*?"

"Shut your filthy mouth!"

"Whoa!" He pretended to stagger backwards. "Got yourself a temper, boy. Didn't your daddy teach you any manners?"

"You're the murderer!"

"Uh uh. I'm the delivery guy. That's my lot in life, but don't get me started—I am full up on misery. All you need to know is that I deliver things; and I'm delivering one right now."

"Then make your stupid delivery and crawl back into the stupid hole you came from."

Ng pulled out the pistol he'd tucked into the back of his pants and cocked it. "Do I have your attention now? You're the delivery, little man. I'm going to wrap you up in a pretty bow and set you on the front porch—rocking away in that ridiculous chair of hers. Rock, rock, rock. That's all she ever does!"

Quietly hunched on all fours, Quigley had returned for round two. He leapt onto the railing, hissing and snarling. Perhaps he was looking for another showdown with his favourite adversary, Miss Newman. Instead, he ran teeth and claws into Ng's face. This time Ng stumbled backward, landing in Terri's rocking chair and discharging one shot into the wooden planks of the veranda. While Quigley scampered for his life in one direction, True dissolved into the darkness in another.

"Come back here . . . weasel!" Ng taunted.

He pulled another cigarette from the pack and held it between his teeth. With his other hand he wiped his face—surprised to see red droplets of blood staining his sweat. He spat a wad of brownish phlegm onto the deck and smeared it into the planks with the toe of his boot. "Now there's only four bullets for you, young Truebell. I'm saving one for that demented cat."

Ng got up from the chair and wobbled down the stairs "My word, this is a *hot* town tonight. Too hot to go chasing weasels, or hellcats—four-legged or two-legged—if you know what I mean." He snickered to himself and then spat as he stared into the darkness—past the blue spruce, through the white picket fence, and up to a green army surplus tent. "Don't you worry about me; I know the perfect spot to rest while I wait."

He exhaled a cloud of smoke and waved the pistol high above his head. "Besides, there's plenty of time. I am, after all, a patient man. Ask anyone." His voice trailed off. "Ask, Miss Newman . . . she knows."

****

Harper stopped what she was doing and turned to Sydney. "Did that sound like thunder?"

Sydney laughed. "Boom!"

Harper switched off the burner and removed the pot of boiling water.

"No, *s'ghetti* for supper?" Sydney watched as the pot cooled.

"Let's play a game first." Harper widened her eyes and smiled. Sydney perked up. She loved games. "You go hide and I'll come and find you." Sydney squealed and clapped her hands.

"Oh, but be extra quiet." Harper explained the rules for this new game. "Can you do that?" Sydney drew an imaginary zipper over her lips while her little legs wiggled with excitement.

"Okay, go! Find the most secret place you can." Sydney padded off wearing her princess tiara and carrying her magic wand. Harper knew all her hiding spots. She picked up her cell and called Finn.

"Help."

CHAPTER SIXTEEN

Dallas slotted the dirty dishes into the dishwasher and wiped his countertops. He couldn't believe his good fortune—a woman had broken bread with him—albeit under tenuous circumstances (her life being in peril and all); but still, of her own accord she had sat in his special chair—the one with the shiny chrome armrests and the yellow vinyl seat cover.

Once the Hungry Man frozen dinners were piping hot, he rolled into place beside her with what he dubbed his police scanner chair. It was just an old office chair someone had tossed out and he had rescued it. Once he replaced the castors, levelled the seat, taped up the dozen or so rips on the arm rests—*it was as good as new*—he told Terri with pride. She smiled.

Tomorrow he would stop by Debbie's and ask for some recipe books, a pan or two, and some extra cutlery; scavenged plastic from leftover takeout meals were fine for him, but with a house guest a "spork" didn't cut it.

"Terri?" He listened for a moment and then stepped into the living room to get her attention.

"Coffee? Tea?"

The room was dim and still. As he leaned over to switch on the table lamp an arm from the shadows reached out to stop him.

"Hot blazes!" Dallas leapt backwards into the kitchen.

"Boo!"

Dallas grabbed his heart. "Terri, on any other night that might be funny—"

"How about now?" Rand Jared Ng switched on the light. "*Oh, Dallas!*" he mocked, "*You got a better getaway vehicle than that bicycle of yours?*" Ng laughed and waited for his wry humour to sink in.

"Not to worry, Mr. Weaver. I brought my own transportation. Perhaps you've heard of it? It's called a c-a-r." He stuck the pistol in Dallas's face. "Don't look so surprised. I know Miss Terri told you all about me—but don't you dare believe a word of it. Now, move."

"What have you done with Miss Newman?"

"My, you're a formal old stiff. You mean, Terri? My old lover? The one who spurned my affections and drove a dagger through my heart? *That* Miss Newman?" He held up a scarf stained with blood. "For now, she's where she needs to be; soon, she'll be where she ought to be." Ng poked him with the gun. "It's a very simple riddle, Dallas. Just think about it—I know you can get it."

Dallas sunk to his knees and let out a low, rumbling groan.

"Holy smokes! It's the critter from the Black Lagoon!" Ng clutched his sides in a fit of staged agony.

"Okay, that's enough big fella." He smacked Dallas on the shoulder with the barrel of his gun. "No drama queens allowed here, Mr. Weaver. Up you go. And, don't get any ideas about dying on me. I'm not done with you, not by a long shot." He shoved the gun under his chin "Get it? A long *shot*."

CHAPTER SEVENTEEN

True kept low as he crossed the yard; his form melded with the darkness and the safety it provided. His vantage point offered up an outline of Harper, bathed in a soft glow as she talked on the phone. He released his breath in a series of shallow bursts, unaware he'd been holding it. True crept to the edge of the tent and opened the flap.

"Boo!"

CHAPTER EIGHTEEN

"Can't this tub go any faster?" Finn thumped his fingers on the dashboard of the car. "Remember: shots fired, Onyx Ave, Terri Newman's house. Sound familiar?" *Right below Harper's house,* his expression added.

Sonny pushed the pedal to the floor and flipped the switch for the siren and the lights. With Finn bracing himself against the passenger door, Sonny roared out onto the opposing lane of traffic. He glanced over at Finn and with a look that said, *You asked for this.*

From the driveway of Dallas's house, Ng could see the lights of a police car rocketing up the hill from the valley floor. "Looks like company's coming, Dallas. Let's leave 'em a message, shall we?"

Ng pulled Terri's scarf from his pocket and tied it to the trunk of the maple tree. "It ain't an *old oak tree,* but it'll have to do. He struck the hood of the trunk with his fist. Can you hear me, Terri? *It's been three long years. Do you still want me?"*

"It has been longer than that, Dallas, but *fifteen* detracts from the original beauty of the lyrics. I worry it makes me sound desperate. Any thoughts?" Ng held the car door and then shoved him into the back seat. Dallas struggled to breathe. Duct tape covered his mouth, his nostrils flared, and the back seat began to spin. He closed his eyes and prayed for a quick death.

"It's time to fly the coop, Birdman!" Ng hit the gas and reversed out of the driveway. "You know, I do love that pond of yours. Let's spin by and do that skinny-dipping thing." He threw the car into Drive. "Or, in someone else's case, a little heavy dunking."

He winked at Dallas and gestured toward the trunk.

"Come on, Dallas. You sing while I drive." A faint sound escaped from the trunk. "Hey, hey! Did you hear that, Dallas? She still wants me." He lit a fresh cigarette, sighed, and tossed it into the back seat. "Smoking will kill you, Dallas, but I wouldn't worry about that."

CHAPTER NINETEEN

"Now you say, *boo who?*"

Sydney stuck her head out of the tent.

"What are you doing out here? All alone?" True crawled past his sister into the stuffy tent. He checked every corner and under every pillow.

"I playing a game. Mommy said to hide somewhere secret."

"This isn't it!" True was trying hard to protect his family from a maniac, but in a tent?

Sydney giggled and lowered her voice, "Mommy thinks I'm in the closet. She so silly, *Toobell.*"

She snuggled closer to her brother. "Close the flap, so he can't find us."

"Don't you mean *she?*"

She shook her head.

CHAPTER TWENTY

Finn checked his cell. He had one incoming call and two missed calls: one from Harper and one from someone named Debbie Dowd.

"Go ahead." It was Verna.

"We have a fix on your request, detective."

"Okay, let's have it—" He pulled out his tattered notepad.

She paused. "It's the same guy who took the picture."

"Say again, Verna. I think we've got a bad connection."

She raised her voice and repeated the message. "It's the same person. It's Rand Jared Ng."

Finn closed his eyes. "Do you realize what that means, Sonny?"

"It means he was at the pond the entire time." He looked over at Finn. "We've got a predator on our hands and I'll bet he knows Terri Newman."

Finn checked his missed calls again. He showed the log to Sonny. "Is this the girl Harper's son is hot after?" Sonny shrugged his shoulders. "One of us needs to pay more attention when we're interviewing people."

Sonny nodded. "Yes, you should—boss."

"Verna, patch me through to Margaret Lamb. She's Terri Newman's lawyer friend."

Sonny edged the car over to the side of the road and took out his own phone. "Want me to follow up with Harper? No?" He teased. "How about the kid's girlfriend, a Miss Dowd, I believe?"

Verna chimed in on the car radio. "Did you say Dowd, Sonny?"

"10-4, Verna. The detective wasn't sure who she was." He laughed.

"Her name's Debbie Dowd. Her father is Dallas Weaver and she believes someone may have abducted him. Unfortunately, she couldn't provide a good description of the abductor, or the vehicle he was driving; just that he headed in the general direction of Rundle's Pond. And she's been calling all evening, demanding someone investigate this *travesty*, as she put it."

"An abduction is a travesty? That's a first."

"No, Simpson! The travesty is that she's had to make *repeated* calls about it and this made her late for her *Adult Children of Divorced Parents Support Group* meeting."

Finn borrowed the car radio. "And she's the *daughter* of Dallas Weaver?"

"10-4, detective. Hang tight for a moment, I've got Ms. Lamb on another line. I'll patch her through in two jiffs. By the way, there was no one home at the Newman house. The officer who responded thinks people are still keyed up from the Halloween incident."

"Not a chance, Verna. Tell him to sweep the house again." Finn muted his phone. "Something's wrong, Sonny. Dallas Weaver is the birdman and the guy with the surveillance equipment. I met him at Harper's this morning.

Verna transferred the call and Finn lit into Terri's attorney friend. "Rand Jared Ng. You said you didn't know him."

"Correction," said Margaret. "I stated I'd never met anyone by that name. There is a difference, Detective Yung."

"Yes, ma'am. It's called lying by omission and obstructing my case." Finn kicked at the dashboard and cursed. "Ms. Lamb, while you and I are playing legal footsies, people . . ." He put the phone in a chokehold and shook it. ". . . real people are in real danger here."

"This isn't a game, detective, unless your name is Ng. And until you figure out that much, I can't help you," she yelled back.

Sonny pulled the phone away from Finn. "This is Officer Simpson, Ms. Lamb. We understand and we're on the same page, but we need your help. Where do we go from here?"

"Haven't you wondered what was significant about Rundle's Pond?"

"Sydney Salmon almost drowned."

"Wrong. It's because Terri Newman *didn't*. This was never about that little girl; she was incidental; nothing more than collateral damage. It's always been about Terri."

Finn's veins bulged on his neck. "Verna, we need some backup out at Rundle's Pond."

"Sonny? Do you know how to catch a snake?"

"I know how to skin one." He reached down and lifted his pant leg to show Finn his boots. "Rattlesnake. This fella tried to bite me the last time I went hiking in the badlands."

"You hike?"

Sonny shrugged as he shoved the car into gear and sped off toward Rundle's Pond. "I also crochet and do the Watusi. I'm what you call a multi-faceted, strong, yet tender, 21stcentury man."

****

Harper tried Finn's cell once more—it went straight to voicemail. *Where could he be?* Beads of perspiration were forming on her upper lip. It was time for action.

"Sydney . . .? Come out, come out wherever you are. Come on, baby, Mommy needs to find True, and Finn, and Miss Newman . . ." It was a burgeoning list.

Ten minutes later, a harried, desperate-looking Harper slowly peeled back the flap of the army tent. She shone the flashlight against the tent wall; her hands were shaking.

"Boo!"

"Argh! You got me." Harper stared at True, tightly holding his sister, their pupils immense in the dim light. "I guess you both got me."

Sydney giggled at this. "I betted you was *s'prised* when I wasn't in the closet?"

"You have no idea . . ." Harper groaned with relief. "Want to go for a ride?" Sydney jumped to her feet and lifted her arms.

"Where to?" True's voice betrayed his nerves.

"Let's start with Mr. Weaver—when we find him, we'll find Miss Newman, and when we find Miss Newman—maybe we'll find Detective Yung?"

CHAPTER TWENTY-ONE

Ng ground his Crown Vic to a stop at the entrance. The park lights shone on the hairpin pathway that curved toward the water's edge. "Mood lighting," he said. "I like it."

"Okay, old man, haul your butt out of my back seat. You've got some digging to do." He tore the tape off Dallas's face. "You're looking purple, buddy. Remember, I said *no dying.*"

"Please don't kill her."

Ng slapped his hands against the rear fender. "Why does everybody think I'm a killer? It's annoying!"

"Because you are."

"No! No!" Ng stomped his feet on the ground. "I ain't never taken a life."

"You take people's will to live. It's the same thing."

"Oh, semantics! Get the shovel out of the trunk and dig before I shoot you and your *little* cohort, Miss Newman!"

Dallas stumbled to the trunk and opened it. Terri's swollen eyes and bruised face stared up at him. She was bound and gagged and her skirt was torn. "Out of the way, birdbrain!" Ng grabbed Terri by the legs and flopped her onto the ground. She hit hard and moaned. He reached in and grabbed a shovel. Dallas retched.

"Don't look at her!" Ng pushed him to the front of the car and flipped on the headlights. "Dig."

"Why?" Dallas wept. "To what end?"

"To what end?" Ng stopped. "Because I said so! Because I never figured the old cow would make it. Because she should have drowned—along with the kid—like a two-for-one coupon." He pounded his chest like a great silverback gorilla. "Because I want to get on with *my* life! Because you have no idea what that woman did to me. Because it didn't matter that her court case was dismissed—in my favour. Because I couldn't even earn a living after that. Do you know I had to crawl back to my stepfather—for a job? I became a delivery man—*for dead people*. How do you think that made *me* feel? Lousy!"

He took a short timeout and smoothed his countenance. "If I understand you correctly, you're asking what is the point of *burying* her?" More time passed as he pondered this. "Perhaps you're right. Perhaps she does need to return to the murky waters from whence she emerged—dragging that limp noodle of a kid with her. It might help give me closure."

He folded his arms and sighed. "And what a glorious day that was, Dallas! For the life of me, I don't know why I was favoured. I believe it was kismet—that, or the gods felt I'd suffered enough and it was Terri Newman's turn—who can say? Anyhow, one day I got lost making a delivery and when I stopped to ask for directions, who should I see? None other than my old lover, Terri Newman, strolling around the pond without a care in the world." He placed a hand over his heart.

"Oh, stop that, Dallas. Old fool. No need to get all wrinkly every time I say Terri was my lover. Besides, it's not like she'll ever bed an old grizzly like yourself."

Ng lit up and took a few quick puffs. It was time for another shot of nicotine. "And to think it wouldn't have been possible without the help of the hottie's delinquent son and his little sister, Sydney Ella." He jabbed Dallas. "Did you catch that? Her cute little name sounds like Cinderella." Ng finished his smoke and flicked it onto the gravel.

"Anyhow, back to your death-time story." He cuffed Dallas on the head. "Stand up straight, boy! Just because I'm doing a decent thing by baring my soul, doesn't mean you get to pass out during story time. Listen up, old man! There ain't no fairy godmother coming to the rescue in this story—she's dead, boy." Dallas hung on the shovel and pretended to listen.

"That's better. Anyhow, I'll be totally honest with you, I wasn't prepared; I had to improvise. That little girl sunk below the water so fast, I almost felt bad for her; all alone, trying to rescue the Little Mermaid I tossed into the cattails. Dumb and dead dumb. Besides, who in their right mind leaves a kid sitting unsupervised by the water?" He rubbed the bristles on his chin. "I have no regrets about doing it. I think it served the mother right. Do you know what I mean? Some people should never be parents—"

He picked up a pair of work gloves and pointed to the dozen sand bags that lay beside a nearby work shed. "Okay, I'm bored. Let's do this."

Ng sized up his frame. "I read you as a three-sand-bag-kind-of-guy." Dallas slowly straightened. "Come on over, buddy." Ng waved the arm holding the pistol. "You'll see . . . it'll be fun."

No sooner than Ng had secured the bags around Dallas's waist, he pointed to the water. "Get in there, my tall drink of water. It's time for your baptism." Dallas stumbled head first into the cattails and when he found his footing he was anchored in decades of muck and debris that lined the pond.

"Work it! Work it, fireman! You can do it!" Ng bellowed his encouragement.

Around forty feet off shore, Dallas vanished from sight. "What?!" Ng shrieked in disbelief. "Is that it?" A few bubbles broke the surface and then—nothing—not even a sad plea for help. Disgusted with Dallas's pitiful end, he spit and walked back to the car.

"Good thing I saved the main course for last, Miss Terri Newman, because the *dessert* in this restaurant was a colossal waste of time."

Ng unzipped his pants and relieved himself, arcing a stream of hot, acrid-smelling urine over the rear fender of the car. "It is so darn peaceful here tonight." He listened to the sound of his pee as it splattered against the dirt. "Can you smell that, Terri? Tell me, does it remind you of a rainforest?" He finished and gave himself a shake.

"That's okay—no need to respond—I'll imagine it for the both of us."

He stooped for the body he'd tossed behind the vehicle; there was nothing but gravel, clumps of dirt, and grass. He got down on all fours and felt around in his own feculent, wet mess. She had escaped her bonds.

Ng ran back to the water. The bubbles had dissipated; the

surface of the pond was pristine. He took off his gloves and threw them to the ground. "Not this time, Terri Newman!" Ng kicked off his boots and dove into the water, swimming out to where he expected to find the body of Dallas Weaver suspended in death. Deeper he dove; still nothing. He broke the surface of the water, gasping for air. Exhausted, he trudged back to shore.

"Boo."

It was the last sound he heard before the glint of the steel shovel caved in his skull.

CHAPTER TWENTY-TWO

"Look, Mommy! There's a ribbon on the tree!" Harper struggled to unclasp her seatbelt and raced into the house. "It's empty," she called back to True. "Do you know how to turn on Mr. Weaver's police scanner?"

A hand crept onto her shoulder. *I'm dead*, her pale face said. She slowly turned around.

True stood behind her holding Sydney in a vise grip. "Yeah, you flip these two switches." He showed her and they listened to the radio chatter. It was focused on Rundle's Pond.

"What'd they say about a dead body?"

"They said two dead bodies."

****

Harper was so tense she could barely drive straight, but with True's help, she found the pond. She pulled the car to a stop before the park's entrance and switched off the motor. The pond was still a bend away; up a tiny hill, and then down to the water, the day use area, and two dead bodies.

"Maybe you should wait here with Sydney." Her face was ashen.

"No way, Harper! I coming." Sydney squirmed out of her car seat and climbed into the front between her mom and brother. Her little jaw was defiant.

Harper conceded and they skirted around to the far side of the activity—away from any dead bodies. "Let's hold back for a minute." She needed time to let her eyes adjust to the darkness. She sat down on a park bench that overlooked the pond and waited.

"There's a lot of commotion down by the water."

True noticed it too. "I can move closer for a better look."

"Not with Sydney!" She reached for her daughter just as True set her loose. Free from his control, she tore off like a wild hare: zigging and zagging over rocks and bumps, her antennae focused on one person.

"Sydney!" Her mother hissed. "Get back here!" It was no use. The flashing emergency vehicle lights and the pitch of night confused Harper's vision. It was like chasing a shadow.

****

Terri was standing over Ng when the headlights from the police cars bathed her in a bluish cranberry mist. She dropped the shovel as Finn shot out of the car and ran to her side. She slumped to the ground, a crumpled mass of cloth-covered skin with twisted bits of duct tape hanging here and there. "Sonny! Get an ambulance! Get some blankets!" He knelt to the ground.

"Is he dead?"

Sonny walked over to Ng and gave him a kick as he searched for weapons. The body moaned. "There's your answer, Miss Newman."

"Is it finished?" She was treading fear so deep she wasn't sure a bottom existed.

Sonny knelt and wrapped a blanket around Terri's shoulders. He looked over at Finn. They both understood—it was just beginning.

CHAPTER TWENTY-THREE

Terri sat motionless and stared out at the water. "Dallas is gone. Is it my fault, Finn?"

"There's more than enough blame to go around, Terri. It's no one's fault."

She tried to stand and flopped back to the earth. "I have no fight left in me."

A wet wrinkly hand reached toward her. "So, stop fighting and give me your hand."

"Dallas?"

"It takes more than three sand bags to torpedo this old bird." He dropped two cattails on the dirt. "Old army trick," his voice shook. "You breathe through them." He waited for her to take his hand.

She pulled herself up and wrapped her arms and her blanket around him. "You were never in the army."

His teeth chattered as he laughed. "Okay, maybe I saw it in a movie."

"Oh, my! What's this?" Terri felt the warmth of little fingers touching her leg. "Up?" the little voice asked.

Terri waved off Harper as she and True came crashing down the bluff. Sydney clung to Terri's neck. "I know you."

"Yes, darling, we met this morning at your house. Remember?"

"Uh, uh." Sydney shook her head and pointed to the water. "Out there."

CHAPTER TWENTY-FOUR

Two days later, Ng's stepfather reported a missing transportation van from his funeral home. On the advice of outside legal counsel, he performed a thorough audit and discovered a body was also missing. Finn shook his head when he heard this and sent a silent thank you to Ms. Lamb.

Rundle's Landing also expressed a collective sigh of relief. The police had caught the villain and folks could return to their normal lives. That was the easy part. The challenging part was bringing Ng to justice. He was, after all, a patient man. A patient man who had no plans on going easy. No way. No how.

****

The birdman returned to his tree from which the crimson leaves had fallen. But this time, he brought a friend.

"Pass me the tripod, Mr. Weaver."

"Let's see what you're looking at." Dallas adjusted the binoculars and yanked them back from his eyes.

True hid his face. Across the road was the newly transformed Cynthia Dowd, granddaughter to Dallas Weaver. She had broken up with her image as Harley Quinn and her boyfriend, Wyatt, but she'd kept the bat and was practicing swings in her backyard.

"No way!" Dallas's grandfatherly instincts bristled.

They climbed down from the tree: True in a pair of old sweats his father had once worn; Mr. Weaver looking awkward in his form-fitting, *but not yoga*, pants.

"Give me those binoculars." He pretended to roughhouse

True. "That's my granddaughter you're ogling."

True laughed. "I don't even know what that means."

Dallas wrapped his arm around him and squeezed. "If you want to gain the affection of a young woman, you must first understand that she's more than eye candy."

"But, I love candy—"

Dallas gave him a swat on his behind and pushed him toward his granddaughter's home. "Go. Talk. No touching!"

True sauntered around the side of her house. He glanced back, a little for support, but mostly for approval, then unlatched the gate to her backyard. He picked up a stray softball lying on the lawn and tossed it into the air.

"Batter up?"

****

"You're a good man, Dallas Weaver." Terri rested her head against his chest as the gate across the street clicked shut.

"Yes, I am." He turned to the full-bodied woman at his side; the one whose name seemed to always linger on his lips. "Lunch?"

She nodded and took his arm. "Please tell me we're using real knives and forks today?"

He winked. "Harper invited us for lunch." Terri pinched him.

"Hey, yoga boy, are you planning on wearing those to lunch?" She raised an eyebrow.

"I love you—*that*—I love *that* about you." He hadn't meant to say those words, or at least not to say them in such a reckless manner while standing exposed in his yoga pants for all the world to see. "You never miss—anything—about—things like that," Dallas stuttered. "But I was wondering if you'd miss me. Do you think you might—one day?"

Debbie Dowd shuffled her feet and cleared her throat, impatient in her pink peony blossom slippers as she tried to catch her father's attention. "Okay—maybe later." She set a box of pots and pans on his doorstep and retreated.

Terri gazed at him. "If you're planning on making a move, it's now or never, birdman. Neither of us are getting any younger—especially you."

He pulled her close. "I promise to miss you until the end of time."

"I know you love me. Now, kiss me, you old fart." And he

77

did. "I bet your night vision goggles never saw that coming."

He blushed. "I may have seen more than I told you."

Terri shook her head. "I think lunch can wait."

CHAPTER TWENTY-FIVE

Harper answered the door and her smile faded. "Oh? Detective—" She stopped short of inviting him into the house.

"I take it you weren't expecting me." He shuffled his feet as he stood on the landing.

"No." She latched the screen door behind her and stepped out. Small heaps of leaves lay scattered around the yard, randomly punctuated by little boot prints. The rose bushes had shed the last of their petals and the welcoming smell of coffee no longer drifted from her house—once so intoxicating for him. Harper pulled her sweater tight around her body.

"I wanted to make sure you were okay," he said.

"The kids are great."

Finn reached into his pocket and pulled out a small evidence package. "Here's Sydney's other shoe and her toy mermaid." He placed the items in her hand. "We found them when we dredged the pond."

She ran her fingers over the mud-stained shoe. "How much evidence did you need?" The furrows in her forehead deepened. She handed back the plastic mermaid with the green fins and the pink hair. "This doesn't belong to Sydney."

Finn turned the little toy over in his hands and then slipped it into his pocket. "My mistake. I thought she liked mermaids."

"With a passion, but this one isn't hers." Harper folded her arms. "Give it to Verna."

"Verna?" He gave her a puzzled look.

"Sure. She can add it to the collection she has on her desk." The chill in the air sent a shiver down her spine, but Finn didn't move. "Was there something else?"

"He's being transferred to a forensic hospital—tomorrow."

"What happened to the criminal charges?" She pursed her lips to steady the quiver in her chin. "Even you, Finn, must realize he's only pretending to be crazy."

The wind kicked up a handful of dead leaves and tossed them at Finn. He shook them from his clothes and raised his hand to remove a petal snagged in Harper's hair. She turned her face and brushed it away before he could touch her.

"I see you're hurting, Harper, but I don't know what else to do."

"Kill him." She stepped into the house and pressed the door behind her.

CHAPTER TWENTY-SIX

Sonny was anxious to talk to Finn when he returned from his meeting with Harper. "How'd everything go?"

Finn undid his holster strap and let the gun drop onto his desk. He stared at it. "Sonny, did you know I've never fired a gun in anger?"

"How about in desperation?" Sonny casually stepped over to the desk and picked up the gun and holster.

Finn rubbed his face and laughed. "No need to worry about that. I don't have what it takes."

"Everyone does—under the right circumstances." Sonny opened a file cabinet and stowed the weapon. He gave the drawer a quick shove and locked it tight, dropping the only key into his shirt pocket.

"Where's Verna? I want to see those transfer papers on Ng."

"She's working on them."

Finn punched the desk. "Now, I said!" The room quieted as everyone turned to watch him, his knuckles red with jagged patches of broken skin and blood. "What's the matter? Haven't you people ever witnessed a little police work?" He kicked his chair and let it roll into the middle of the room where the cracked green leather seat spun in circles.

"What's all this ruckus about?!" Verna crossed over to his desk and handed him the transfer papers. She pulled in close, maybe a whisker's length away from his face, and with her minty cigarette breath, she let him have it. "Bring it down a notch, detective. Your behaviour isn't helping anyone." She retrieved his chair from the middle of the room and rolled it back. She pointed to it and said, "Sit."

Finn paced a few steps like a petulant child, then stuck out his chin and straightened his collar. His witty comeback account was suddenly empty. He swiped a glance toward the pack of cigarettes tucked in a fold of her skirt. "Those things will kill you."

Sonny smirked, *Rookie mistake.*

"I'm sixty-seven, twice divorced, the kids never visit, and the dog ran away. I don't drink—at least not enough for this job—and on top of all that, I get the pleasure of working with the likes of you and Simpson." Her hands were on her hips. "So, get off my case, grow up, and let me enjoy the one vice I have."

Sonny walked over and swept Verna off her feet with one gigantic bear hug.

"Put me down, Santino," she screeched, "before you become part of the #MeToo movement!"

He gave her an affectionate peck on the cheek and gently placed her back on terra firma.

"That's better." She unruffled her feathers and admonished both men with a reproving glare. "Now, get to work! That Ng ship sails in under twelve hours and none of us want that boat to float."

****

Ben rested one foot on the side of the tub as he laced up his shoes. But mostly because it was the perfect spot to admire his reflection in the mirror that hung above the chipped, green enamel sink. He was a new man: short cropped hair, a sweet pair of Maui Jim sunglasses resting atop a good-looking head, and wearing one *sick* leather jacket.

Sydney picked up on the changes straight away. Her sharp eyes captured every nuance, and when Ben strolled into the kitchen to pick up True, she scanned him seven ways to Sunday.

"Where's the old Ben?"

Harper looked up from the sink and greeted him with a pleasant expression. "Wow, Benjamin! You're a handsome sight."

He glowed with pride as told her about the crazy film project he'd made with his friend, Fraser, and the whopping $1500 someone had paid him for the film rights. He was quick to edit out the embarrassing bits: True's wet pants and Big Bertha.

"Is that legal?" Harper frowned.

"I hope so." He popped a Skittle in his mouth. "All I care is that the money was real. I had the bank check it out."

"Your dad thought the money was counterfeited?"

Ben nodded.

"It sounds like one lucky break." She turned back to the dirty dishes, watching Ben out of the corner of one eye.

He whistled. "That was my best Halloween ever." Amnesia was his new middle name.

Harper drained the water from the sink and finished wiping down the countertops. She lifted Sydney from her highchair and herded her upstairs where they met True bounding down, two steps at a time. In his own way he was as GQ-looking as Ben, dressed in a worn-out t-shirt and sporting his usual shaggy hair. It pleased Harper to think *he had something in the making*. She flushed crimson as she remembered the source of those words—Miss Cynthia Dowd.

"Ben's here." She collected a clean bath towel from the linen closet.

"Okay."

"He's got money." She left it at that and headed toward the bathroom. He swivelled to read his mom's expression, snagged his foot on the bottom step, and toppled head first into the kitchen.

"You drunk?" Ben chided his friend.

True circled the kitchen table, checking Ben out from all angles. "You on the take?"

"Aw, you're jealous." He popped another Skittle into his mouth.

"Am not."

"Are too."

Their banter carried on until True threatened to mess up Ben's hair. He pulled away, patted down his locks, and retold the film story: wet pants, Big Bertha, and all.

"You can't sell my personal experiences without my permission," True raised his voice. "That's invasion of privacy."

"We blurred out your face," Ben snipped. "TV stations do it all the time. I don't understand; why is this such a big deal for you?"

"Show me the video and I'll decide for myself." True demanded.

"I can't—we sold the rights."

True snatched the Maui Jim's and perched them on his head.

"How do I look?"

Ben stared at his new sunglasses camouflaged between mounds of clumpy, brown hair. He curled his lip and pulled out his cell. "No guarantees—but maybe there's a copy."

True slouched against the kitchen counter. "Why do you even bother to say that?" he said. "I know one of the Moore misfits kept one."

Ben held up the phone and showed him the text. "Tell him he's got five seconds, or I'm coming over to beat on him."

The phone binged. "Got it."

The boys huddled around the kitchen table; reliving the Halloween from hell, up close and personal, and in living, Technicolor splendor. It memorialized every cringe-worthy detail and now it was in the hands of a—what, thought True? *A weirdo, a blackmailer, a producer from America's Funniest Videos?*

"That night just keeps getting better."

"Sorry, True. It was a no-brainer way to make some easy coin."

"Yeah, yeah." True walked over to the fridge and poured himself a stiff one: chocolate milk shaken to a frenzy. He wiped his upper lip. "I need the original back."

"How?"

"Give back the money. And then some—whatever it takes."

Ben hung his head and shuffled toward the door.

"Aren't you forgetting something?" Harper plucked the expensive-looking pair of Maui Jim's from her son's head and handed them to Ben. "Benjamin, everything you do in life has consequences. Some things you can never take back." She gave him a hug. "Try to remember that, son."

He nodded. "Come on, True, let's go strangle Fraser." He opened the front door.

"Works for me." She flipped off the kitchen lights and switched on the porch light. "Be home by—" Harper couldn't bring herself to dole out a curfew in the same old way. She turned to admire her son as he waited on the threshold. "Just make sure you come home."

"I can do that." He smiled. She gave him a thumbs-up gesture and marched upstairs to tuck little Miss Salmon into bed.

CHAPTER TWENTY-SEVEN

Dallas couldn't seem to take his eyes off Terri as she slept—on his bed. It was well past supper, and he couldn't recall where the time had flown. He laughed. Yes, he could. Terri's lashes fluttered, and she wriggled around in the sheets to face him.

"How long have I been sleeping?"

"Not long enough." Dallas brushed her cheek with the back side of his hand; *no calloused fingers for this lovely creature.* He sighed with contentment.

"Did you tell Harper we weren't coming for lunch? Or dinner? Maybe we can make it for breakfast—if we hurry."

Dallas swung his legs out of bed and pulled on a regular pair of khakis. "I'll make us some coffee, maybe some eggs, two slices of toast, some bacon, a few hash browns, and some sliced-up oranges." He mimicked the shocked look on her face. "And, yes, I'll give Harper a call." He kissed her and picked up his cell.

Harper answered after the second ring. She was out of breath. "Are you okay?" he asked.

"Oh, Dallas, I'm so glad you called. Sydney's having an asthma attack and I can't get my car to start."

"Terri's with me, sweetheart. We'll be there in two minutes." He hung up and grabbed the keys for Terri's car. "Terri, we have to go. It's Sydney."

Clothes materialized out of thin air and slid over her body. "Ready!" Once a firefighter, always a firefighter.

****

Dallas sped through each colour of traffic light: horn blaring and emergency lights flashing. Terri strapped herself into the front seat next to Dallas, while Harper bounced from side to side in the back, balancing Sydney on one knee. Her baby's lips were blue. No one spoke, and positively no one criticized Dallas's driving. Whenever he didn't slow for a corner or swerved around a vehicle, both women clung to a door handle, the dash, or a roof bar. It was their right foot, pumping the gas pedal and willing the car to fly, that spoke to them. There was no time to lose.

The car bounced off the curb as it jerked to a stop in front of the emergency entrance. Harper squirmed her way out of the bucket seats, Sydney in tow, and ran through the sliding glass doors. Nurses at the ER desk immediately waved her into the first trauma room. Nebulizers spilled from drawers, a quick history was taken, and asthma medication flowed through the mask placed over Sydney's mouth. After a few minutes, she relaxed her grip on her mother's arm and settled into her treatment. Slowly, her lips changed from a deep violet to mauve to pale pink.

"Deep breaths, Sydney." The nurse with the pretty brown eyes encouraged her.

****

Terri waited on the sidewalk while Dallas parked her car. She reconciled their ETA with her wrist watch—house to hospital in three minutes. "Not too shabby, birdman." She felt the tension easing in her shoulders.

"Excuse me." The male orderly addressed Terri. She stepped aside as he wheeled a patient over to the far sidewalk for a cigarette. His head was bandaged from the tip of his nose to the crown of his head, leaving just enough space for two sunken eyeballs. Terri watched his hands tremble as he held a lighter to his cigarette. His orderly had stepped away to help another patient.

"Need a hand . . .?" Terri started to say until she caught sight of the handcuffs.

The man lifted his head. "You must forgive my gruesome exterior. I was the victim of a hit-and-run—with a shovel."

Terri backed away and motioned for his orderly. "Where's Security?"

"Supper break." He reached down and removed the drool from Ng's lip. "You can hardly consider this poor fellow a threat."

He pulled on the cuffs and showed them to Terri. "He couldn't hurt a fly even if he wanted to."

Ng lolled his head to the side furthest from the orderly and winked at her.

She watched in horror as the orderly lit his cigarette and he attempted a few puffs. When he finished, the orderly stubbed out the smoke and spun the wheelchair away from the curb. He nodded to Terri as he passed, coming close enough for Ng to extend his index finger and lightly run it across Terri's thigh. She blanched.

Dallas hurried across the road. "Thanks for waiting." He gave her a hug.

"Terri?"

She couldn't open her mouth to speak.

"I understand, love, but this hospital is fantastic. Trust me, nothing terrible will happen to Sydney." He kissed each of her hands and pulled her toward the door.

CHAPTER TWENTY-EIGHT

Ben and True stood outside the Moore residence: committed, resolute, and sweaty. Fraser answered the knock and just as quickly tried to slam the door. True wedged his boot between the frame and the door while Ben lunged at the opening and together they pushed their way into the house.

"Talk to me . . ." Ben said.

Fraser slunk into the nearest closet and began to whimper.

"Listen, punk, I told True's mom we were coming over here to strangle you. She said, and I quote, 'Works for me.'"

Fraser screamed, "It wasn't me! It wasn't me!"

True looked at him in disbelief. "I don't care how loud you get, man. Give me that video, or die."

"Yeah." Ben echoed, "Die!"

As Fraser started to howl and flail his arms, Everett emerged from an adjoining room. He strutted over to his brother and with rehearsed precision, crushed his torso against the wall until all the air bled from his lungs.

"He doesn't respond well to your type of persuasion—too gentle. I know, I've tried." Fraser stopped yelling. He gasped for air and mouthed obscenities at his brother. Everett ignored him. "Besides, *Part Deux* is what you really want."

"You're insane, both of you," said True.

"Clinically, only me." Everett confided. He yawned and pointed to his brother. "He's the wildcard." Everett grabbed Fraser by a fistful of hair and straightened his body. "This noodle tried to overstep his authority by posting that idiotic film on YouTube." His eyes narrowed. "But, did he consult with me? Even once?" Everett made a fist and struck his brother in the solar plexus. "I had a plan, a vision. Now I'm out $1500, paying off Ben so he can look like a grade A buffoon in his knock off Maui Jim's, and a pleather coat from Wal-Mart."

"Oh, don't look at me like that, Benjamin! I've seen where you shop and I also know that your dad relieved you of most of the money." He teetered on his feet and held up an arm pretending to have a drink from a bottle. "Your old man's a booze hound and you're a loser."

"Just give me the video, Everett, and spare us the lecture."

Everett sized up True. "It'll cost you."

"We figured that. How much?"

"It's not a dollar figure." He toyed with pile-driving his brother once more for good measure. "I need something original for my portfolio, something priceless—bring me a lock of Ng's hair."

"What do you know about Ng?"

"I read, Truebell. Just like you, only not comics." He opened the door and shooed them out.

****

"What do you think?" Ben dropped his shoulders and shoved his hands deep into his pockets.

"I think he's a serial killer in the making. I also think he doesn't know a thing about you, or your dad."

Ben cocked his head to one side, grinned, and looked up. "So, how do we get some hair?"

"We don't, we make Everett think we did." True patted Ben on the back. "Nice jacket."

CHAPTER TWENTY-NINE

Harper tapped her cell. Sydney was resting, but she needed another round of meds before they'd release her. She waited for True to answer.

"Hey, kiddo." Her voice was weary. "I'm calling to let you know that I had to take Sydney to the ER tonight—"

"—no, no worries. She's much better. Dallas and Terri drove me." She smiled into the phone. "Remind me later to thank you for signing up for Driver's Ed. I think Dallas missed that class in school."

"—Oh? He learned to drive on a brontosaurus? I'll tell him you said that, but from personal experience, he's definitely more of a raptor." She hung up and pulled the covers over Sydney's arms. She had stabilized, so staff had moved her into one of the regular ER cubicles.

A young volunteer rolled by with her refreshment cart. Her name tag read Connie, and she had personalized it by dotting the *i* with a red heart. Harper liked her straight away. "Mrs. Salmon, may I offer you something to drink or read?"

"Just coffee, thanks." Harper stood up and stretched. "But I'll get it myself."

Connie nodded and stepped into the next cubicle to make the same offer. "Nurse?" She called out. "This patient needs help."

From beneath the curtains, Harper watched as a pair of hairy legs stood in a tangle of clear plastic tubing. She waited a moment for staff to respond, then nosed her way through the curtains.

"Hold tight, I can fix that for you." She crouched and coiled the plastic tubing into a large circular ring and hung it on the wall outlet. "That should make things easier." She reassured him with a smile. His eyes crinkled at the edges when they met hers. She squeezed his arm and left to fetch her coffee.

As soon as she returned to Sydney's cubicle, the ER volunteer swooped through the curtains and in a hushed voice demanded to know what Harper thought she'd been doing. Harper pointed a finger at Sydney. Connie shook her head. Next, she pointed to the adjacent cubicle. This time Connie made two fists and shook them. "Old Mrs. Grimsby in 2A called him a masher!"

"What's a masher?"

"I don't know, but it must be really awful if Mrs. Grimsby called him that. She doesn't say that about just anyone." Connie thought further and added. "Usually she doesn't speak at all."

Harper lifted a corner of the privacy curtain. The hairy legs were missing.

"He's gone," she mouthed.

"He's padlocked to the bed now."

Harper's voice rose with concern. "What do you mean, *now?*"

"Earlier this evening, an orderly lost track of him, so we had to enact a Code Yellow. That's the code we page when a patient goes missing, and boy, oh boy, there will be you-know-what to pay for this." She wrung her hands.

Harper shuddered. "Where did you guys find him?"

"Back in the ER! Mrs. Grimsby spotted him first and pressed her call bell. He was wheeling himself up and down the aisles, peeking inside the cubicles."

"How odd." Harper positioned her body closer to Sydney.

"Stay clear of that one, Mrs. Salmon. He's dangerous. *They* say he's the one who shot Thelma Ryerson's cat."

"She lives one street over from me!"

The volunteer's eyes got wide. "What if it *was* him?"

"Mommy?"

Harper's sleepy girl had removed her mask and held out her arms. "I better now. I wanna go home."

"Okay baby." Harper bundled her up, sickened by the thought she may have engaged with a cat killer. She decided to secret herself and Sydney out of the ER and found Terri and Dallas sitting in the foyer.

"How's our girl?" they bounced from their seats, eager to hear a good report.

"Oh—" Harper made a stink face. "Let's leave first and talk later."

She turned and bolted for the door. Terri was hot on her heels.

CHAPTER THIRTY

"Okay, Mr. Ng, let's have a look under those bandages." The ER doc slipped on a pair of blue latex gloves and cut away the meters of gauze wrapped around his head. "The nurses tell me those scratches on your face have been giving you some trouble." Ng nodded.

The doctor peered at his wounds. "Your head trauma is healing well; there's a little redness on your cheek, but I see no signs of infection." He peeled off the gloves and tossed them into a waste bin. "Did you also have a run in with a cat?"

"Something like that."

The doctor tapped Ng's cuffs with his pen. "Looks like the cat won."

"At least I still have both of my legs." Ng raised his hand, cocked an imaginary gun, and pulled the trigger. "So long, Puss 'n Boots."

The doctor studied Ng as he completed his paperwork. When he finished, he handed it to the intern. "He doesn't need to be here."

She pointed at the cuffs and informed him that Ng was awaiting transfer to a forensic unit in the city—tomorrow. The doctor shook his head. "That's not going to fly. I'll give Rundle PD a call and tell them to come and get him. We don't have time to babysit when the waiting room's swamped with patients. What's our count?"

She flipped to the ER room assignment sheet and did the math. "Thirty-two."

He snorted and glanced sideways at Ng. "He'll live through

one night in custody."

Ng raised the middle finger on his right hand.

"You know, there's no coming back from where you're going, Mr. Ng."

"Great advice, doc. Make sure to remember me in your will."

He nudged his wheelchair forward and butted up against the doctor. "Nobody leaves a mark on me without paying for it: not a hellcat, not this stinking town, and not you."

The doctor grabbed the arm rests on Ng's wheelchair and shoved him back toward the bed.

"Whoa, my double-chinned, tub-o-lovin', quack-tor!" Ng's face twitched. "That hurt. Can I get a witness?" His face hardened. "I'll remember that at my hearing, doc—the one where I'm never charged—because they find me not criminally responsible and the crazy board grants me an absolute discharge. Oh, yes, I'll remember you." He cocked his finger and aimed at the doctor as he stormed out and bellowed for Security.

The shaken intern watched from the curtained entrance, clipboard in hand, as Ng chanted, "Bad air out; good air in." When he realized he was alone with her, he sidled to the end of the bed using his feet as propellers. He crinkled his eyes and smiled. "You people got me all wrong, pet. I'm the victim here. I endured a head injury." He felt for the sutures and the shaved patch of hair. "Come on over and I'll show you. Better yet, let's you and me sneak outside for a quick smoke."

"Better yet, how about you take a quick ride with us?" Finn eased the terrified intern to one side, giving Sonny space to take Ng into custody.

"There's a pooper for every party." Ng rolled his eyes. "Lucky me, I get two."

****

True checked the time—it was running out. He and Ben hurried along the same route they'd followed Halloween night, the one that lead straight to Miss Newman's house. The massive spruce trees still spooked True; their shadows engulfed most of her yard. As they sprinted down the street, Terri's car pulled into the driveway.

Ben's brain was running on breakfast leftovers. "Mr. Weaver has old hair. Do you think he might lend us some of the darker strands?"

True made a face. "Would you want your hair back after the likes of Everett and Fraser got through with it?"

"You're right, *lend* is the wrong word—maybe he'd *give* us the hair?"

The boys bounded up Terri's front steps and pounded on the door. Terri hid behind it and called out, "Yes? Who is it?"

"It's us, Miss Newman. Ben and True."

She opened the door, surprised to see them. She waved off Dallas who was standing behind her, his .22 cocked and ready.

"Holy smokes! He's got a gun!" Ben jumped behind True.

"Dallas! Put that away. You're scaring the boys." She opened the door wider and ushered them into her foyer. Terri un-cocked her own gun: a single-action Colt .45 six-shooter "Peacemaker" and set it on the sideboard. The boys alternated between staring at the gun and staring at Terri. "It belonged to my great-grandfather."

They continued to stare.

"He's dead." She spoke with a measured tone, the way a parent explains a hot stove to a child. "I didn't kill him, in case you're wondering. My family passed it down to me." She nudged Dallas for help. He was in bliss and the object of his bliss owned a really cool gun. He couldn't wipe the grin off his face, or understand a word she said.

"Have you boys ever heard the saying, *never bring a knife to a gun fight?*" Terri looked in Dallas's direction. "Or, a pea shooter?" The spell broke, and the boys giggled. She patted Dallas on the rump and asked everyone to take a seat in the living room. Terri folded her hands in her lap and waited for someone to speak. A few minutes of silence passed and she looked at the clock. "It's kind of late for a visit."

"True's in deep … poop, Miss Newman. He needs your help and Mr. Weaver's hair—but only the dark parts." True stretched out his leg and kicked Ben underneath the coffee table.

"Ouch! It's true, isn't it?"

"Thanks to who?"

Dallas formed his fingers into a pyramid. "I'm intrigued. Go on." Minute by minute they peeled back the layers of the story: soggy pants and butt-licked candy. "Those brothers are queer in the head." Dallas offered his forensic analysis.

"Most likely." True conceded. "But what if the second video

has the hard evidence we need?"

"And all you need to do is bring this Moore kid some hair?" Terri sized up Dallas's head with a worried look. "Did he say how much?" The boys shook their heads.

She walked over to a curio cabinet in the far corner of the room and removed a small hand-carved chest. "I'm not proud to say this, but ..." She opened the box and removed a plastic bag filled with dark hair. "If worse ever came to worst, I intended to frame Ng. I always suspected he wasn't right in the head." She handed the bag to True who cradled it as Terri's mantle clock chimed midnight. It was definitely too late to turn back.

Dallas stood. "I think I'd better tag along and keep the boys safe while they make the exchange."

True hid a smile. "I've heard you can drive."

"But he's got to stay in the car—no questions asked," said Ben.

****

Terri locked the door behind them. Her house stirred with rancid anticipation when it should have been enjoying lavender-scented dreams, just like her. She parted the curtains over her kitchen sink. Harper's house lights winked back and seemed to ask, *What are you waiting for, Terri? The kettle's on the boil.* She locked up her gun, grabbed a warm sweater and a flashlight and picked her way through the darkness to Harper's back door. She hoped there was no more need for a Colt .45, or a pea shooter, tonight.

CHAPTER THIRTY-ONE

Dallas eased Terri's car into Opal Meadows. Household security lights blinked on in a steady, predictable fashion as he coasted to a stop in front of the Moore residence. Ben was a sink hole of sweat. He cleaned his face with the sleeve of his new jacket.

"You've got something on your—" Dallas motioned to Ben's nose.

"It's tannin—from the leather!"

Dallas spun back around and gripped the steering wheel. "It's something all right," he said.

True stood outside the car and banged on the hood. "Let's go, man!"

Together they approached the door; no lights shone from within and no sleepy security lights had awoken to blind them in a searing spotlight. "What if they've gone to bed? What should we do then?"

"WAKE 'EM UP!" Dallas honked the horn.

True tucked his ears into his shoulders and winced. He pressed the doorbell. Soon the muffled sound of shuffling feet approached the door. It was Everett wearing a blue velvet jacket and little else.

"Got the item I asked for?" He stepped out onto the landing and scanned the street. "Who's the fossil in the car?

"My guardian angel." True held out the baggie.

Everett backed into the house as a blast of cold air whistled up his backside. "Can you guarantee that's his hair?" He reached for the bag.

Ben looked away. "Don't you need a dress code or something to live in this neighbourhood? Put some pants on, dude. Who raised you? A pack of wolves?"

Everett clutched the lapels of his father's best smoking jacket. "If you must know, I thrive on freedom from clothing, it helps me think."

"About what?"

True's eyes widened and he stared at Ben. He shook his finger back and forth, *Focus, Benjamin. We've got bigger fish to fry.*

He held out the bag again. "Do you want it or not?"

"Yeah, yeah, take it easy." Everett tossed him the flash drive. "*Part Deux*, as promised."

"This better be worth it, Moore."

They ran for the car. "Where to, fellas?" Dallas asked as he peeled away from the curb.

"Rundle PD, Detective Yung." True steadied his hand as he clutched the flash drive.

****

Finn yawned. "It's time to head home, Sonny. Tomorrow's another day."

"Let me get this clown into lockup and I'll join you."

Ng shuffled through the squad room, rocking his head and drooling at the night shift. He paused beside Verna's desk. The desk sergeant gave him a shove and told him to keep moving.

"I was just admiring her mer-mammals." He smirked. "I used to have one, but I misplaced it Maybe you've seen it? Green fins, pink hair?"

Sonny came up behind him and commandeered an arm. He opened the steel cage and felt Ng's resistance. "What's the matter? Too good for the likes of you?"

Ng made a half-closed bedroom-look with his eyes. "I was just wondering which chamber had encased our Miss Newman. She's a former *lover* of mine." He licked his lips. "It'd be romantic to have the same cell—for old time's sake. That's all."

"You are one sick puppy, Ng."

"Thank you." He knelt before the cement bench slab and inhaled. "Yes, I believe that's her unique blend." Satisfied with his discovery, Ng yawned, picked up his blanket and lay with his back against the wall. "No funny stuff, fellas—I sleep with one eye open."

Sonny was reluctant to let go of the cell door. In reality it was already tomorrow and Ng's boat was one step closer to setting sail. *Red sky in the morning, sailor's warning.*

****

Terri gave three soft taps on Harper's patio door and called out her name. She listened for the sound of her footsteps as they padded toward the door. Harper switched on the patio lights. "Terri? What are you doing up so late?"

"I saw your lights and took a chance."

Harper pulled her sash and tied it. "Well, come on in and make yourself at home. I was about to make a cup of tea before I head to bed."

Terri searched Harper's face. "Do you have any idea where True and Ben are?"

"No, not really. They said something about confronting Everett Moore. Are you familiar with that family?" Harper slid into an empty kitchen chair, rested her head on her chin.

Rundle's Landing was new to Terri, but not so new she wasn't aware of the eccentric family who lived in Opal Meadows. She nodded.

"As I understand things, the boys paid Everett a visit on Halloween night before coming to your house."

"This much I know."

"And there's a video Ben made, or helped make, and sold for money, and now True's frothing mad." She massaged her neck. "Kids never change, do they?"

Terri reached across the table and touched Harper's arm. "On that account, where True and Ben are concerned, I believe you're wrong."

Harper rose from her chair and pulled two china tea cups from the cupboard. "These were my grandmother's." She held them out for Terri to admire. "She brought them from Prince Edward Island—only broke two. I've broken a dozen or more." She lit the gas range and set the kettle on the burner.

"I admire your home." Terri cast an approving eye at the snapshots and colourful magnets that lined the fridge; the little herb garden of thyme, rosemary and basil thriving in old earthenware pots, adorning the ledge above the kitchen sink; the ceramic bunny cookie jar sitting cock-eared by the stove.

The kettle sang. Harper suspended two chai tea bags into the teapot and set the lid on to steep.

"So, tell me, where's my wayward son?"

"Not to worry, Dallas is supervising."

For the first time in many months, Harper howled with laughter, joined by Terri with a stream of tears running down her face. The two women sat back and basked in a rare moment caught between worlds, knowing there may never come a better time to leisurely sip tea. As the night wore on, they chirped and chattered about love and family and home. There'd be no talk of justice or revenge, strands of hair, or Colt .45's. Those things had no place at this table. Not tonight.

****

By the time Dallas and the boys reached Rundle PD, Finn had long since convinced Sonny to call it a night—their tanks were empty. The night sergeant stationed at the desk hunched forward, debating whether to take a message. In the end, he decided they should come back in the morning.

Heads hanging low, the trio trudged over to the foyer. Dallas slowed his pace. "Did you hear that?" Far down the hallway, a melancholy voice crept along the green tiled walls.

"I think I hear singing." True hummed a few bars.

"No, it's a radio," Ben said.

True nodded. "I bet they leave it on for the prisoners." He looked at Dallas—pale, numb-looking, waiting for the other shoe to drop.

"Oh, sure," he joked. "It's just a radio."

"You have bat-sonic hearing, Mr. Weaver." Ben clapped him on the back and sang as he sprinted toward the car. "Tie a la la ribbon on the la la tree."

"Let's go home, Mr. Weaver." True held the door for him. Dallas rubbed the goose flesh on his arms and quickened his pace.

CHAPTER THIRTY-TWO

It was 2:00 a.m. by the time Dallas deposited the boys with Harper and swung around the block to Terri's house. She was just walking up the steps as he pulled into the driveway. "Back so soon?" She teased. "How went the espionage?"

He looked drained. His eyes were red-rimmed and some mysterious force had sprinkled his gaunt face with salt and pepper bristles in the few hours he'd been away from her. Dallas drew her into his arms, willing the song out of his head, but it was no use. The melody carried him to Ng's back seat where Terri was in the trunk, bound and gagged—and he was helpless—again.

"Did you know . . .?" Terri placed her finger tips on the soft curves of his mouth. "No more news tonight; it can wait for the morning." She slipped her arm around his waist and led him inside, to her bed.

****

"You're staying and that's final." Harper put her foot down. "Tell your dad he can take things up with me *tomorrow*." She absolutely refused to entertain Ben heading home at this late hour. "Now, off to bed—both of you."

She fanned them upstairs with her arms, then found her own bedroom and sprawled on top of the covers. As she rested her head on the pillow, she gave thanks for good husbands, good sons, good friends and neighbours, and the miracle she called Sydney. It didn't matter what the morning brought; everything was okay now, and that was enough.

CHAPTER THIRTY-THREE

Finn lay back in bed and stared at the ceiling; he listened to the seconds tick away on his windup alarm clock. He glanced at its face, it was the witching hour. Finn covered his head with a pillow, unsure why he'd bought a model with luminescent dials. For an insomniac, the exact amount of missed sleep was better left unknown.

An image of Ng flicked through his mind. His preoccupation with this case had left him drained; he was way beyond any professional responsibilities. Late at night, he found himself imagining the worst for Harper and Miss Newman. These thoughts and others even worse, steam-rolled back and forth across his mind, wearing a deep trench, until the first rays of morning sifted through his bedroom curtains. Still, he found no peace. He tossed his pillow onto the floor and rolled out of bed, gasping as he stepped into a frigid shower.

Sonny fared no better after a night's sleep of 'no sleep.' His once dapper silver locks hung in stringy grey ribbons across his forehead. He splashed water on his face and ran a toothbrush over his dentures. No time for a shower today. He slipped on a fresh pair of dress pants and clean socks and tucked in his smartly pressed navy-blue shirt. He splashed on his favourite cologne for a little extra camouflage and headed out the door.

The men pulled into the parking lot seconds apart and stared at each other, too tired to acknowledge how absurd it seemed. They'd left in the dark and returned in the dark—other than that, what was different? Sonny's cologne?

"Get much sleep?"

"No."

Sonny handed Finn a cup of coffee. He'd picked up two double-doubles on his way to work. "Donut?"

"Yeah, sure." Finn snagged one from the bag. "Thanks."

Sonny grinned. "Never doubt the power of chocolate sprinkles and caffeine on an empty stomach and no sleep."

"Amen to that, brother." It was 5:17 a.m.

****

The Salmon household sprang into action as soon as Dallas and Terri banged on the door with a gusto only reserved for police raids and emergencies. Curtains flew open; beds were abandoned, still warm and rumpled; brushes ran through hair, and teeth were smudged clean with a finger before everyone squeezed down the stairs to answer the door.

Terri was bright and cheerful. In fact, she sparkled.

"Good morning, this house!" She greeted everyone as she let herself into the kitchen. "Coffee?" She waited for the grunts and then set about brewing a pot. Dallas tried to help, but soon realized his place was in a chair by the corner. He reached over and tickled Sydney; her laughter reminded him how much he'd already missed as a grandfather.

"Do we have time for breakfast?" True squeezed past Terri to make toast for Sydney.

"We'll make time." She pulled out three mugs and filled the table with plates, knives, cereal bowls, and glasses—enough for a small army.

Harper dashed into the room and gave Terri a friendly hug. She surveyed the table with delight. "Thank you for this."

"Where's Ben?" She poked her nose into the living room.

"He left before dawn." True picked up the hot toast and spread it with a thick covering of jam and peanut butter. Sydney smiled and dug in, wearing most of it on her face.

Dallas translated for Harper. "He had a covert op."

"Sometimes his dad can be—wary."

Terri made a serious face. "Is that a good—thing?" She followed True's lead.

"When it comes to Ben?" He laughed. "Absolutely."

Harper flipped her hair into a loose ponytail that hung to her mid-back. Dressed in a slim pair of leggings with an oversized hoodie, she didn't look much older than her son. "What's the game plan, team?" She took turns looking from True to Terri, to Dallas.

True tilted his head toward Sydney, "*Oday ouyay hinktay hattay YdneySay houldsay taysay ithway randmagay ndaay randpagay?*"

"Isn't it a little early for Latin?" Harper blinked the sleep from her eyes and gulped down a big swallow of coffee. "This is fantastic, Terri. You're hired."

Sydney pushed up the tip of her nose and snorted. "I know what he said, Mommy. It's piggy talk!"

"We can't today, my little one. Grandma and Grandpa have plans. So, you will have to come with us." Harper tweaked Sydney's nose and wiped the jam from her chin.

True tried to object, but Dallas interrupted him. "He's at Rundle PD, Harper."

Harper paused, as if to respond *What on earth are you talking about?* But then you could see that she remembered and her face fell. "I forgot. How'd that happen?" She looked over at Sydney and asked True to take her upstairs and pack a few toys and books for the day.

"Is *that* what you wanted to tell me?" Terri took Dallas's arm. He nodded.

Terri found her own resolve. It was time to come clean. "I ran into Ng at the hospital last night." Harper caught her breath.

"It threw me for a turn. What could I say—to either of you?" She fumbled in her pocket for a tissue and looked at Dallas. "It happened while I was waiting for you to park the car. An orderly brought him alongside the curb—in a wheelchair—to have a smoke, no less! I know this will make little sense, but I didn't recognize him under all the bandages. I even offered to light his cigarette."

"That must have been awful for you."

"It was. It terrified me that you and Sydney might run into him. Imagine if that had happened?"

"I can't imagine—" She grabbed the coffeepot. "Top up—?"

Dallas remained silent. He started tapping a spoon against the side of his mug; his eyes were glued to Harper. It wasn't long before she cracked. She replaced the pot on the warmer, put one hand to her forehead, and one to her abdomen. "Okay, I saw him, too."

"I knew it." He slapped a palm against one knee. "I thought I was losing it; both of you acting like you'd seen a ghost."

"More like a ghoul, my friend."

Terri's cheerful mood dissipated like a puff of stale smoke. "It's hopeless, Dallas. He'll probably get off, spend time in the psych ward, but little else. He's done his homework."

True touched his mom's shoulder. "—and that's why we have to get this flash drive to Detective Yung."

Sydney scampered onto her mother's lap dragging her over-stuffed backpack behind her. "I ready to go," she sang out.

CHAPTER THIRTY-FOUR

Terri's station wagon lumbered into the Rundle PD parking lot twenty minutes later. The group piled out of the car single-file and headed through the entrance whereupon they demanded to see Detective Yung. They were on a mission and formed a circle around the desk.

"You missed him." The night shifts sergeant let them know. The posse was unmoved. "He's gone to the city with a prisoner." Their circle tightened. "People—read my lips—he won't be back until late this afternoon, if then. Come back tomorrow." He signalled for the day shift super to take over. Then he left.

The new officer was likewise curt and to the point. "If you folks have no further business, I must ask you to leave."

Dallas took the lead. "We have new evidence in the Ng case—"

The voice of the day shift super had a timbre that rumbled low and uneasy; it also had the firepower to pin back wobbly earlobes. "I'm sorry, sir," he said. "That file is no longer active. Mr. Ng was transferred to First City Psych about an hour ago. What happens now is beyond our control."

True pulled out the flash drive. "I'd like to leave this for Detective Yung."

"I'll be honest with you, kid. It won't change the outcome."

"But what if it proves his state of mind? What then?" True's voice was tight with emotion.

"Listen, I recognize who you are and why it's important. But you'd have to get a judge to issue an order, and that's not likely to happen for at least ninety days."

"Ninety days?" Harper picked up Sydney.

"Yes, ma'am. The court ordered a ninety-day psych assessment."

Terri gripped the worn, wooden countertop. "Are you saying we have no other recourse?"

"Miss Newman," he called her by name. "I'm no lawyer, but a lawyer is what you need, and likely more than one to contest this case and bring new charges."

Harper clawed at her clothing and fell into Dallas's arms. "I can't breathe." Her body slumped to the floor and Sydney screamed.

****

Harsh white lights flooded her surroundings. She squeezed her lashes close together. Harper's head throbbed to the sound of the wailing siren as it reverberated off the metal-clad frame of the ambulance. She covered her ears and cried.

Terri held her hand and pressed a cool cloth to her face and neck. "Everything will be okay, love. Just breathe."

****

True couldn't reach his grandparents, just as Harper had said. He took his mom's cell and began to go through her contact list. By the time he got to the R's, he was getting nervous: every person before had either begged off, or hadn't answered. Mrs. Ryerson picked up on the first ring. He explained the urgency, trying to calm the crackling in his voice, and asked if she could watch Sydney.

Thelma Ryerson lived below the Salmon house, and two doors north of Terri Newman. She was a most agreeable old gal, but she preferred the company of cats to people. Ever since the placement of Mr. Ryerson in a local care center, her house had become a lonely reminder of how full her life used to be. Having a child to care for was just what her oven mitts had ordered.

"My dear boy, bring her at once." She set to work preparing the house for little hands: ornaments moved to the top shelf, cleaning products safely tucked away, and knives secured.

"That should do it!"

Thelma curled a few loose strands of hair around a finger and poked them back into her bun, then pinched her cheeks to a rosy glow. Feeling sublimely satisfied, she rummaged through the cupboards for the perfect recipe: strawberry shortcake. Her old bones were happy as they danced to a new song.

****

Prisoner Ng slouched in his seat, restrained with hand cuffs and leg irons for the hour-long ride to the city; his face was another matter. He had frozen his face into a Cheshire cat grin; the muscles in his cheeks taut and twitching. He held the pose throughout the ride, throughout processing at the admission unit, and into his final placement in a private room. Finn watched him through the small window slit in the door, curious how a sane person could bear such physical discomfort.

Sonny nudged Finn to one side and looked for himself. He toyed with the idea of banging on the door. Instead, he waited for Ng to notice him. Sonny's eyes became soulless pits of misery wanting nothing more than to consume the maggot before him. Ng turned away first—his pasted grin not so convincing anymore. Sonny stepped back from the door.

"Let's go home."

"What was that all about?"

Finn narrowed his eyes to mimic Sonny's expression. As they left the building, the afternoon sunlight washed over his face and the devil mask was gone. Sonny "Santino" Simpson was back: a smile on his lips and a swagger in his hips. Finn studied his partner-in-crime for a sign, a crack in his veneer, something that said, *Gotcha, Yung! You're so easy! Wait 'til I tell all the guys back at the station. You'll never live this down. Squirrel!*

"You're a scary old fox, Simpson."

"Tell me about it." He slammed the door tight on the police van. "Let's go! Finn and I have a couple of hot dates tonight." He winked at Finn, folded his arms across his chest, and dozed off.

CHAPTER THIRTY-FIVE

Muted voices floated in and out of Harper's awareness. In the back of her mind, she wondered how long she could stay disconnected from this reality. The short answer was, not long.

True pried up an eyelid and frowned at his mom. "I know you're in there—"

She forced herself into a sitting position and scowled at the worried lines on his face. "You are way too young to look so old." She scrunched his cheeks with her palms, released her grip, and watched them snap back into place.

"What happened?"

Harper shrugged. "I think everything just caught up with me, but I'm fine now. I am. I had a good cry and I'm over it—really."

"The student intern wanted to send you over to First City's psycho ward—Miss Newman almost fainted and Mr. Weaver went up one side of him and down the other for even suggesting it." He held back a smile.

"No need to worry." Harper patted his arm and smiled at her baby boy, *mommy's back.*

He laughed out loud. "Oh, I wasn't."

"Where's Sydney?"

"Mrs. Ryerson has her, and just so you're prepared, I don't think we'll be getting her back any time soon." True took extra care to describe Thelma's preparations for Sydney: the strawberry shortcake and how "in your face intoxicating" her house smelled.

The crease lines in Harper's face softened and her muscles

relaxed. "Thank you."

"Anything for you, Mom." He opened the small, bedside closet and collected her things. "We should hurry. Get dressed." It wasn't a direct order, but close. Harper let it slide as a "hurry-up-quick" request. She slipped on her leggings and hoodie while True kept a close eye on the door.

"Is something going on out there? What happened to Dallas and Terri?"

True gave her a sly grin. "Security escorted them off the premises—and they may or may not still be looking for me."

Harper's jaw dropped.

"Okay, not!" True used his *happy* Sydney voice. He knelt to slip her shoes onto her feet.

"Wrong foot."

True looked at the shoe and compared it to her foot. "Just kidding." Harper gave him a noogie and finished getting dressed.

True tugged her by the arm out into the hallway. "Wait." She turned toward the nurses' station. "The doctor needs to discharge me first."

"No, you're good." He continued pulling her toward the foyer. "Trust me."

Outside, his eyes swept the parking lot for Dallas and Terri. On the second sweep an arm poked out from behind the naked potentilla shrubs. It was Dallas. "Run!" he yelled.

****

The Rundle PD van lurched to a stop in one of the underground parking stalls. Sonny shook the cobwebs away and climbed out. He stuck his head back inside looking for Finn. All that remained was the echo of a door clicking shut and a shadowy figure tackling the stairs, two-by-two.

Finn breezed into the squad room. "I need an update. Somebody? Anybody?" Verna filled him in on the two visits by Dallas, True and company.

"Two visits?"

"Yes, they're a persistent bunch. True wanted to drop off a flash drive, but the day shift super told him to sit tight. Said it was too little, too late."

Finn rotated his head until he heard a chorus of cracks. "Unfortunately, he's right on that account."

Verna walked back to her desk and filled a bag with colourful, plastic mermaids. She handed it to Finn. "Here," she said. "Give these to the kid when you check in on her mom."

"Why would I check in on her mom?"

"Because she snapped, and then they hauled her away in an ambulance?"

Finn tucked in his shirt and slipped on his jacket. "Verna, will you let Simpson know I had to clock out early?"

"Sure thing." She reached up and straightened his tie and flattened a stubborn cowlick. Taking hold of his collar, she turned his face toward hers. "She *wants* what she had, son, but that's not what she *needs*. Comprende?"

He tried to look shocked, but it was no use. He grabbed the bag and bumped into her with his hip. "You're a good hunk of brie, lady—just a little moldy."

Verna swatted at him as he jumped out of the way. "Make sure you tell the little brat they're from her Auntie Verna."

She sauntered back to her desk and bathed in a moment of contentment; then she flipped her pen in the air and pushed her chair under the desk. "Time for a smoke," she said.

"Geez Louise, Verna, how many smoke breaks are you planning on taking today?"

"This is my last one, fellas." She removed a cigarette from the package and tossed the rest in the trash. "I promise."

CHAPTER THIRTY-SIX

"It feels like I've been asleep for a lifetime." Harper mussed her hair and pressed her face into the frosted car window. She reached forward and squeezed Terri's shoulder. "I didn't appreciate how well you coped by yourself for so long."

Terri shrugged. "It was part of my routine, no different from eating or sleeping." She maneuvered her car into Harper's little cul-de-sac and coasted to a stop outside the front door. The high from their daring escape had waned. No one moved.

Harper looked at True. "Do you suppose Mrs. Ryerson will mind watching Sydney a little longer?"

"She said for you to take all the time you need." His serious teenage eyes pinged on hers. "Trust me, she meant it. She's ready for Armageddon."

Harper gave a nervous snort. "Well, barring the end of the world, I'd like to watch whatever's on that flash drive of yours. Anybody else interested?"

****

Harper unlocked the door and slumped into the first available chair. "I don't understand this," she said as she rested her forehead on the kitchen table, arms dangling past her knees. "I'm wiped."

"It's the two Ativan tablets they gave you." Terri picked up the dirty dishes from this morning and set them in the soapy water to soak.

"Two?" Harper parted a few strands of hair and peeked through them.

"I know, right?" True joined the conversation. "Since when are you heavy into drugs and stuff?"

"Stuff? What stuff?" She was wide awake now.

True winked over at Terri. "They asked if I knew whether you had regular BMs. I didn't know what that meant, so I said no."

"No?!"

"They may have given you a little something for that, too." True leaned over and kissed his mom on the cheek. "You'll be squeaky clean and passing soap bubbles in no time."

Harper's head slipped back onto the table and she sighed. From her skewed angle she could see the bottom half of a man standing at the door. "We've got company." She didn't bother to lift her head.

Dallas swung the door wide and a blast of chilly air rushed in with Finn. Harper shivered and raised her head. "No offense, detective, but do you bring Old Man Winter with you wherever you go?"

"No, sometimes I bring the heat." He chuckled and found a seat.

"Why are you here?" Harper asked him.

"Verna said you needed me."

"Huh?" She raised her head and tried to grasp his meaning. It was hopeless. *Later*, she yawned, *much later*.

He set the bag of mermaids on the cupboard. "These are from her."

True inserted the flash drive into the USB port on his laptop. "It's good you came, Detective Yung. We can watch this together." He pressed the play button and adjusted the volume.

Harper reached for Terri's hand as the shaky filming began. It was outside Terri's home: she was rocking in her chair and they could see a grey tabby's tail switching back and forth on the railing that surrounded her veranda. The cat was ready to strike.

"I loathed that cat."

The next few minutes were of Ben ransacking her trays of lemonade and iced tea and ending with him swiping the entire platter of candy and hurdling over the handrail. "Nice moves." True caught the stink eye from his mom. "For a juvenile delinquent . . ." Terri grinned. Those rebels had stolen more than her candy and iced tea: they'd stolen her heart.

True covered his eyes as the film featured him and Ben staggering about the lawn, smashing the rum bottle they'd swiped from Harper's liquor cabinet and stabbing the Crypt Keeper with it—too stupid to notice they were killing a *dead* man. They kicked her No Trespassing Sign and stomped over her personalized grave marker. They were the ones who had decimated her yard. Not Ng.

True dropped his head into Terri's lap. "I am sorry, Miss Newman. Ben and I will make everything right."

"Yes, you will—and I'll help," Dallas said as he watched Terri pat True's head. *I didn't hold your dying father's hand for nothing, son.*

Soon after, the Rundle PD arrived and there was a panoramic sweep of the yard. Everett zoomed in on the drippy-looking Crypt Keeper and then panned out as the Medical Examiner carted him away. Everyone watched as the police seated Terri in a plastic chair, wrists bulging from the zip-locks. Mrs. Ryerson was in the caragana bushes trying to wrangle out her cat, and last to the party was Harper. She materialized from the backyard wearing bunny slippers and a terrycloth robe, and carrying two weapons: a pink mallet and a flashlight.

"You can shut it off, True. This is nothing new," Finn said.

True moved to click on the pause symbol, but his finger slipped and the video bounced to the end. Ng's voice was discernible.

"Back it up." Finn shifted to the edge of his seat. "Okay. Start there."

Harper grabbed True's arm. "Do you suppose this kid hides cameras in other places—like the pond?"

"I don't think so, Mom. He's not that breed of sick."

"Breed?"

"The Ng variety." Finn considered telling Harper how strange Ng's behaviour had been on the ride to the Psych Centre, but figured it might only strengthen her resolve to prove him of sound mind. And, from what Finn had seen, Ng wasn't, and possibly never had been of sound mind.

Harper sat back and watched in horror as Ng threatened her son with a pistol. She motioned to Finn. "Isn't that evidence of a crime?"

He didn't answer but kept his eyes on the screen. The cat leapt off the veranda and seemed to purposely attack Ng—clawing and scratching his face. It was just enough time for True to run and hide.

"I loved that cat." Terri's eyes were brimming.

The gun fired and they could hear Ng taunting True with his remaining bullets. The gun fired again. Ng stumbled into the light from the front porch and wiped the blood from his face.

"That's all of it." True pushed stop and ejected the flash drive.

"Mind if I make a copy?"

"Keep it." True lowered his face and left the room.

"I have to go, too." Harper gave a proper hug to Terri and Dallas and wobbled her way up the stairs to her bedroom.

"She's on drugs." Dallas picked up the dishcloth to wash the dishes.

Finn nodded. "Where's Sydney?"

Terri explained how Mrs. Ryerson had stepped up and taken care of Sydney when Harper had collapsed at the police station.

"I'm sorry I wasn't there when it happened. I wish I could have helped."

She rubbed the spot on his sleeve where he wore his heart.

"Detective, our pasts are like a patch of Creeping Charlie; we think we've pulled out all the roots; but there's always one seed that sprouts—same place, same time, every year." She sounded resigned. "It's never over, until it's over—for you, for me, for Harper."

"How do you know—?"

"I think it's when you die." Dallas declared in a somber tone, elbow deep in soapy dishwater.

"No! That isn't it."

Terri twisted up a damp dish towel and snapped it at him. "It's the little things: like the first time you forget to lock the door behind you and it doesn't scare you to go back into the house, or you sleep through the night and it's the morning sun that wakes you up and not the sound of footsteps outside your door, or when your heart skips a beat, but it's only because you're lying next to the one you love. Little things."

****

Thelma Ryerson was a happy woman. After hours of playing hide and seek, three tea parties, and a dozen make-believe stories, Sydney curled into her lap and devoured Thelma's family history. The stories behind the old photos entranced her.

"This is my Abe." Thelma touched his picture. "When I couldn't take care of him anymore, he went to live in a special place." Sydney nodded.

"My daddy lives in a special place, too."

Thelma gave the child a hug. "Would you like to see more?"

"Only a little, then I go home." Her honest baby face tugged at Thelma's heart.

Thelma set the heavy photo albums to one side and picked up her phone to call Harper. When Terri answered Thelma explained that Sydney was ready to come home and asked if that would be okay. While they waited for Terri, Sydney spotted a picture of Thelma's cat on the mantle.

"He's beautiful," she squealed. "Where is he?"

Thelma's face saddened. "Someone hurt him and he died."

Sydney patted Thelma on her hand. "What was his name, *Telma*?"

"Quigley."

"I like it." She hugged her. "If it's okay with Mommy, I come back again."

****

The evening had warmed up from the day and Terri decided to walk the short distance to Thelma's house. She cut through Harper's backyard, then into her own and zipped two doors over to collect Sydney. Terri rang the doorbell. As she waited she lifted her face and let the falling snow collect on her eyelashes.

The door opened and a bundled three-year-old, complete with a bonanza-size bag of goodies, waited by the door. Sydney dove into Terri's arms, excited for her to visit with *Telma*. The two women discussed Abe and then what a delight it had been for Thelma to watch Sydney.

Sydney tugged on Thelma's sweater. "Tell Terri about your kitty." She pointed to the photo of Quigley.

"That will have to wait, love. Besides, your cheeks are getting rosy with you all bundled up in your winter clothes. Us two chickens will cluck things over another time." She winked at Sydney and handed the goodie bag to Terri. Sydney held up three fingers and winked back.

Thelma watched them carve out a fresh trail as the first

snowflakes of the season began to fall on their heads. She called out, "Terri, make sure you let Harper know I'm available anytime, and I mean *anytime*!"

CHAPTER THIRTY-SEVEN

Finn stretched to brush away the heavy snow from his windshield. He felt a crunch beneath his foot and spotted a lonely mermaid laying at his feet. She had fallen from the bag and was swimming in an onslaught of fluffy snowflakes. As he picked her up and shook off the snow, it occurred to him that Sydney was still at Mrs. Ryerson's. This might give him a double opportunity: one, to ask Mrs. Ryerson what else she'd recalled from the night in question, and two, drop off a ray of mermaid sunshine for Sydney.

He eased the car onto the snowy roads, signaled right to turn on Greystone Boulevard, and just as quickly spun off into the ditch. His summer tires sunk into the heavy, wet snow and disappeared. He wasn't going anywhere—just like this case.

"Dispatch? I need a tow."

****

The whirling red lights reminded Finn of the disco ball from his junior high prom; it was twenty years later, and he was still standing against the gymnasium wall without a date. He snickered at the irony of it and then waved to the tow truck driver.

In a New York minute he was standing at Mrs. Ryerson's door. She opened it a tiny crack and asked if she could help him.

"Yes, ma'am, it's Detective Yung from Rundle PD. We spoke a few weeks back after the incident at Miss Newman's house."

"My goodness, detective, this has been a most busy day for me." Thelma bustled about, taking Finn's coat and offering him a seat in the living room, close to the fireplace.

"You're not from around here, are you?"

"No, ma'am. I'm a new transfer from the west coast."

"Well, you'll need a good pair of gloves for this weather." She observed the broken skin on his knuckles.

"Yes, ma'am. I'll get a pair first thing in the morning."

Thelma asked if he'd enjoy a coffee or hot chocolate. "My Abe loves his hot chocolate," she said.

"Yes, please." He held up the orphaned mermaid, dripping with melting snow. "I was hoping Sydney was still here."

Mrs. Ryerson looked unimpressed. "You're too late for that, detective. She's gone home."

"And, of course, to ask whether anything else had come to mind."

"No, I don't think so. What have you learned?"

Finn fidgeted, flipping the flash drive between his fingers. He searched her living room. No PC in sight. It was unlikely he could show this to her even if he wanted. "I have a video—"

"A video—?"

"Yes. A young male filmed himself at Miss Newman's crime scene."

"Do tell." Finn had piqued her interest. "How do you take your coffee?"

He described how the camera had been anchored to a tree limb in an obscured location and how it had captured various neighbours, such as Mrs. Ryerson, at the scene.

"And?" She placed a mug in front of him. "I can tell there's more, detective. You may as well fess up. Cream? Sugar?"

He held up the flash drive. "It's something you need to see, Mrs. Ryerson. It's on this."

"Oh, is that all!" She laughed. "Come into my office where I can plug that flash drive of yours into my USB port."

He followed her into the library. Thelma popped it in and hit play. Immediately, happy tears came to her eyes. "Aw, there's my handsome, Quigley."

"Quigley?"

"My cat. Someone shot him—I had to put him down."

"I'm sorry for your loss." His fingers reached to eject the flash drive. "Maybe you shouldn't watch the rest—"

She made a puzzled face. "Why on earth not? You need help

to identify people from the neighbourhood and I've lived here for decades. I know everybody!"

Thelma rested her feet on a small velvet footstool and settled in to watch the video. She identified everyone on the clip, including Everett. Finn lit up when she gave him a laundry list of information she'd gathered about the Moore's. He reached for his pen and scribbled in his notepad.

As the clip grew more intense, Thelma clutched her throat. Quigley sprang unprovoked from the porch, raking his claws across Ng's face. It wasn't too long after that a second shot rang out and Ng staggered into the frame wiping blood from his face.

"Those sounds terrified me." She confided as she shrivelled into her chair. "But, I'm an old woman living alone. I could no more place my feet on a cold floor than peer out into the darkness for a gun-brandishing fool. It wasn't until the next morning when I found Quigley lying on the step—splattered in blood—that I realized the sounds had been gunshots."

"If it helps, Mrs. Ryerson, I believe Quigley's actions saved lives."

She nodded. She was grateful for that much. "It's like something possessed him." Thelma reached for a wooden bookshelf and rapped three times.

Finn leaned forward. "I cannot prove this, but I firmly believe a man by the name of Rand Jared Ng shot your cat."

"Is that the ruffian on the video? Where is he?" She fumed. "He will hear from me!"

"That's not possible, Mrs. Ryerson. He's in custody for a ninety-day evaluation."

"Well, of all the wickedness. I suppose he's over at First City?" She paced about the room. "First, he stalks and harasses Miss Newman for fifteen years, then he finds her and tries to kill her *and* Sydney, *and* he shoots my Quigley." She steadied her quivering lip, "I tell you true, the mere thought of that man makes me want to spit. Do you have any idea how hard it is to spit with dentures?"

Thelma unplugged the flash drive and handed it back to Finn. "You must excuse me, Detective Yung, I'm feeling overwhelmed by this information and I must ask you to leave."

She dabbed a handkerchief to her forehead and took her

pulse. "Please let yourself out."

Finn collected the mermaid and left. He smacked his hand against his brow as he revved the engine. "Stupid, stupid, stupid."

****

Thelma opened her laptop and waited for her search engine to appear. She typed in First City Psychiatric Treatment Centre and jotted down the address and visiting hours; then she searched for the bus schedule from Rundle's Landing to the city. Content with her plan, she set the empty mugs in the kitchen sink, double-checked the doors and windows, and stooped to gather up an ethereal shadow from the floor.

"Bedtime, Quigley." She gave his ghost a kiss and carried him off to bed.

CHAPTER THIRTY-EIGHT

Christmas came with the usual feasting, fussing, and fretting. Cookies were baked, then eaten, then more baked and more eaten; songs sung with lyrics never heard in voices out of tune; and festive lights blinked and twinkled and dripped like melting icicles. That was the good part.

The Christmas *crash* seeped through windows, under doors, and down Santa's chimney pipe; like moisture drawn to an eager sponge. The shiny tinsel lost its luster and pine needles lay scattered across an empty floor, no longer littered with gifts. Overspending invariably showed up in the mail in a plain white envelope stamped *Urgent,* or *Overdue,* or sometimes *Past Due* in brilliant red letters, while overindulgence by the feasting beast, reared its jolly head the next time you squeezed into your favourite skinny jeans. Life always demanded a reckoning.

It was nearing February and the ninety-day-evaluation was close at hand. Finn had received updates on Ng's progress since late November and for the most part, it was the same old thing: spends his time rocking back and forth; has a facial twitch; displays aggressive behaviour one day and then the next is docile and timid, hiding beneath his bed.

Sonny, too, never missed a teleconference with the psych center; always expressing the same concerns: *He can't be that good at playing them. Can he?* He depressed the mute button as he and Finn talked. Finn shook his head. "It doesn't matter what we think." He opened his note pad when the therapist started the meeting.

"Good morning, everyone. We have some new developments to report on Mr. Ng. We're not sure how best to explain this, so I'll just list the changes for you: he's stopped sleeping, he's displaying increased confusion and hallucinations, and he's refusing to bathe or drink water. We ordered a battery of tests—" They listened as she scrolled through his results. "—all of which came back negative: no infection in the blood or urine, no fever, no kidney failure. His heart, chest, and lungs all look normal. EEG was unremarkable. We're at a loss to explain this radical shift."

"And his treatment plan hasn't changed?" Finn asked.

"No, no variation. The only thing worth mentioning is a visitor he had last Thursday—first one ever, in fact—an elderly aunt who was passing through on her way home."

"Did you get her name?"

"Thelma Ryerson. She lives in Rundle's Landing. Do you know her?"

The line went dead.

CHAPTER THIRTY-NINE

Harper darted about the house, checking behind curtains, under couches, anywhere a little girl might hide. "Come out, come out wherever you are," she sang to the empty room. There was a soft skitter of feet coming from the kitchen pantry and Harper leapt to the door and tore it open.

"Mouse!" She screamed, waving her arms. "Mouse in the house!" She grabbed the broom. It darted between her legs and ran into the living room.

Sydney scampered from her hiding spot: a new toy chest from Santa. "Where is it?" She giggled with excitement.

Harper snapped her fingers and pointed to her side. "*You* stay with Mommy!"

"Uh uh. I catch it for you." Sydney crept into the living room, face pressed into the carpet, eyes peeled for any sudden movements.

"Sydney!" Harper gritted her teeth. "Get off that floor at once."

She grunted, but did as her mom said and shuffled back into the kitchen.

"S'prise! Here she is!" She held the golden-brown beast by the tail; its little white feet struggling to find solid footing. "Want me put her back in the pantry?"

Harper opened the patio door. "Let's set him free. He'll be so much happier in the wild."

Sydney wasn't sure, but it was a sunny day and Harper looked testy holding that broom. She dropped the mouse onto the snow-covered flower bed and waved goodbye. "You should know, Mommy, she was a girl mouse." She crossed her arms and rolled her almost four-year-old eyes at Harper. "Did you think of her children?"

Admonished, Harper set the broom aside. "I assumed she was a single girl?"

"Hmm . . . let's hope so." Sydney skipped back to her playroom.

"Sydney Ella Salmon! Make sure you wash your hands."

Harper opened the pantry door. The shelves were overflowing with canned goods, dry goods, and all-in-all too many places for a mouse family to hide. She voted against a thorough sweep, shut the door, and placed a rolled-up mat in front.

"Sydney?" She selected a coat from a hook in the porch, gave it a good shake, and then slipped it over her arms. "Mommy needs a lesson in cats. You coming?"

She scurried into the room, breathless.

"Easy, there, peanut. Catch your breath." Harper rummaged through her purse for Sydney's inhaler. She shook her head no. "You sure?" Sydney nodded. "Maybe a cat isn't a good idea for you." Sydney jumped up and down until Harper threw her hands in the air. "I'm not saying no, or yes." She used her serious mommy voice, "First we talk to Mrs. Ryerson."

"But Quigley's dead, Mommy."

"I know." Harper helped Sydney zip up her jacket and pull on some mitts and a toque. "But I bet you didn't know Mrs. Ryerson used to be a nurse. She knows lots about cats *and* asthma."

"Was she a nurse that *gived* needles?" Sydney's face soured.

"Well, sure, but she gave out ice cream, too."

"Oh, Harper, you coulda told me this earlier. You know I been spending years with her." She tapped her snow boot on the floor.

"I'm sorry. I didn't know needles could scare someone who picks up mice—"

****

They followed the footprints made by *Gladiola*, the little mouse Sydney had named after she'd placed her in the snow. Her tracks led straight to the garden shed.

"See? That's a housing situation one hundred times better than Mommy's pantry." Sydney narrowed her eyes. "Hmm."

Harper's feet followed the well-worn path to Terri's house: the one she trampled each morning and evening, like a jungle beast travelling to its watering hole. She and Terri were kindred spirits now, two souls in lockstep about many things, but mainly to do with Rand Jared Ng.

****

Every day that brought Ng's court-ordered evaluation closer, also painted the hollows of Terri's eyes deeper hues of blue and purple. Sleep evaded her and an old fear had come home to roost. What if Ng was found not mentally competent to stand trial and released eight, ten, or twelve months later? These thoughts crippled her. Within a year he could be free; washed clean of any wrongdoing. Terri felt her life constricting, snuffing out any surviving remnant of the joy she'd recently felt.

One blustery morning, she awoke to find Dallas standing beside the bed, suitcase in hand. She gathered up the covers, suddenly feeling self-conscious and vulnerable. "Is something wrong?" she whispered to him.

"I purchased a ticket to paradise." His eyes were sad.

Terri had heard Dallas tell this story before. "Are you leaving me?"

He shrugged. "I don't want to—but I'll be forced to if you don't get out of that bed. Now, move it before the plane leaves without us."

That was on a Tuesday morning. By Tuesday evening, they'd abandoned the snow, the chilblains, and the sadness for the shores of Mexico. The Pacific waters were calling them to untangle the old and tango to the new. Harper volunteered to keep an eye on things and water the house plants until they returned. *One day*, she reflected, *that'll be me*. In the meantime, she basked in the happiness of her two best friends.

****

Harper wove her way through Terri's yard, past the giant blue spruce trees where bats would soon be roosting, past the veranda, and down her red shale driveway. Something suddenly tweaked Harper's memory; she paused in front of Terri's house and scanned the trees, wondering what had happened to the Moore kid. Was he still making videos? Was he making one now? She stuck her tongue out just in case.

"Harper, you making me nervous." Sydney tugged on her mom's arm and pulled it to her side. "We should hold hands."

That lasted about thirty seconds, then Sydney spotted Thelma's house and tore through the snow banks and raced up her steps. "*Telma*? You home? *Telma*?" Sydney knocked louder and looked at her mom.

Harper tried to peek through the separations in the curtains. The house was dark. "I don't understand, peanut. Mrs. Ryerson said she was home, and I told her we'd be right over." Harper noticed the fresh tire tracks on the snow-covered driveway. "Something important must have come up."

The sky clouded over as they made their way back home, pausing twice more to scour the garden shed for Gladiola. Harper carefully glanced toward the doors and windows leading into her house. All clear. Gladiola hadn't returned, and hopefully she really had been a single girl.

"I don't see her, Mommy. Do you think she's okay?"

Harper looked at her daughter. "You do understand why Mommy wanted a cat?"

"Of course!" She smiled. "Gladiola needs a friend. You're the best mommy, ever." She hugged her mom and trudged inside to kick off her boots and plan a tea party for three: Sydney, Gladiola, and Cat—he'd pick his own name once he arrived.

CHAPTER FORTY

"I can't believe the old gal actually made it inside to see Ng. What do you suppose they talked about?" It miffed Sonny. "I mean, it's not like they ever allowed *us* to visit him. What if she gave him something?"

"Such as?" Finn slowed the vehicle to a crawl as he rounded the corner that had lured him into the ditch this past December. He continued on to Onyx Ave and pulled to a stop in Thelma Ryerson's driveway.

"Poison."

Sonny stepped from the car and mounted the steps to her door. He gave it a good thump. "Rundle PD, ma'am. Open the door!"

"Was that necessary?"

"You bet." Sonny snorted. "She could be dangerous; could be reaching for her 12-gauge shotgun as we stand here waiting for her to answer the door, distracted, as it were, like fish in a barrel."

Finn lowered his voice. "You're distracted, *as it were*, and you watch too many movies. Maybe she should slip *you* something."

"Joke all you want, Yung, but Ng took a serious turn for the worse the day after she paid him a visit."

Thelma appeared from beside the garage, shovel in hand.

"Set that down, Mrs. Ryerson, nice and slow." Sonny unclipped the snap on his hand holster.

"Officer Simpson, do you suppose this snow will shovel itself?"

"Did you *suppose* poisoning Rand Jared Ng would bring justice for your cat?" Sonny hammered a few more nails into her coffin.

"I never hid my identity," Thelma defended herself. "And I most certainly didn't poison him!"

"Be that as it may, Mrs. Ryerson, we need to discuss this down at the station."

Sonny opened the rear door of the police car. "If you don't mind."

"I'm being transported like a common criminal?" She huffed and then stepped into the car. "I want this on record: I'm only doing this to humour *you*, detective. After which, I expect Officer Simpson to apologize as he shovels my driveway!"

****

Verna was busy at her desk when Sonny and Finn escorted Mrs. Ryerson into one of the interrogation rooms. She refused coffee, water, juice—oh, wait, her hand went up, *a nice cup of Oolong Tea with sugar and a skosh of milk would be lovely.*

Verna sent a runner to the coffee shop next door. He came back with a chocolate covered Long John and an extra-large double-double.

"What's this?"

The kid shrugged. "They thought the tea was a joke. This is for Captain Simpson, right?"

"You don't say? For *Captain* Simpson?"

The kid nodded.

Verna lifted the lid off the coffee cup and added a *skosh* of whiskey from the bottle in Sonny's desk. She looked about and then added a second *skosh* for good measure. "I'm sure his *Captain's* pay will cover this."

She tapped on the glass window of the interrogation room and held up the donut bag and cup. "Enjoy your *skosh*!" She smiled. Finn plunked the two items in front of Thelma. She took a whiff and pushed the cup aside.

"Whoever told you that this was *Oolong* has a great deal to learn about tea." Curious, she took another whiff. "However, as Irish coffee goes, this will do nicely." She took a sip and then opened the donut bag. "More surprises? How lovely."

"Shall we get started, Mrs. Ryerson?"

"Thelma. Please." She took a sip of coffee and got comfortable in her chair as she nibbled on her Long John.

Finn straightened his tie and gave her his best concerned-son look. "You need to tell us everything that happened when you visited Ng."

"I don't understand." Thelma searched his face for an explanation. "I only wanted to confront him about my veterinarian bill." She harpooned Sonny with a deadly stare—right between his bushy eyebrows. "Thankfully the detective suggested I bring this!" She rattled her purse at him.

Thelma sorted through the contents of her handbag: packets of photos, grocery store receipts, a floral package of Kleenex, hand sanitizer—non-alcoholic (the other type gave her a rash, she said), two unopened packages of peppermints, which she lay on the table and instructed Finn to help himself, a handful of rubber bands, a nail file, some lip balm, her house keys, and something that looked suspiciously like bear spray.

"You know we don't have any bears in Rundle's Landing." Sonny returned the favour of a stink eye. "And that stuff's illegal."

Thelma ignored him and continued to sort through her zippered compartments. "I was sure I had it with me . . ." Sonny flopped back in his chair and watched the ceiling fan spin. "Ah ha!" She held up a crumpled page. "Exhibit A."

Finn took the invoice from her and handed it to Sonny. The bill was steep—into the thousands. "I should've been a vet." Sonny tossed the paper on the table. Thelma set her cup aside and gave him a sideways glance, *Oh, really?*

Finn kicked the leg of Sonny's chair. "Please continue, Thelma."

"There's not that much to tell. I planned a trip to the centre and pretended to be his aunt. Once I got there, they took me to what they called a *Quiet Room,* and I waited almost fifteen minutes before they brought him to me."

"And no one asked for your identification?"

"No, Officer Simpson, not everyone is as suspicious as you," she scolded him. "And this bottle isn't bear spray it's Poo-Pourri— my own special blend. I'll be sure to make you a bottle as I'm sure your co-workers will appreciate that."

Sonny grunted and returned to cataloguing the goo hanging

from the ceiling fan: dust, fly wings, and spit balls, courtesy of some perp. He was more than happy to leave the questioning for Finn. S*he's all yours, buddy.*

Finn circled her back to Ng. "So, he's in the *Quiet Room* with you—and then what happened?"

"He's insane." Thelma was blunt. She picked up the bill and held it; her eyelashes fluttered. "I didn't want to go . . . it was Abe's idea. He said I should."

"Who's this Abe character?" Sonny rolled his head to one side.

"My husband!"

He swivelled his chair around to find Verna and tapped on the glass; drawing a large circle in the air with his fingers (*Another round!*).

"My apologies."

"As I was saying, Abe thought it was only right I give him a chance and hear his side of the story. So, when he came into the room, I introduced myself and showed him the invoice and a picture of Quigley—I brought the large 8"x10" frame." Thelma unfolded her trademark embroidered handkerchief and blew her nose. "Mr. Ng said *I* should pay *him.* Can you imagine that? Then he rang the buzzer and before staff arrived, he winked at me and told me he'd come calling as soon as they released him."

Verna retrieved Thelma's empty cup and replaced it with a fresh one.

"Thelma, the man is unhinged." Finn went on to describe his behavioural changes and how they coincided with her visit. "Do you understand the danger you put yourself in—not to mention the hospital, and us?"

"Is that so?" She finished her coffee and then stowed away the contents of her purse.

Finn pulled his chair a smidgeon closer. "For the record, did you say or do anything that could have affected his well-being?"

"He said Quigley's death had nothing to do with him." Thelma applied a dab of lip balm. "He laughed in my face when I guaranteed him it did."

"That sounds ominous." Sonny turned from his preoccupation with the ceiling fan and gave Thelma his full attention. "Tell us what you're not saying."

"I told him my prediction for his future. I don't think he liked it."

"What did you tell him?"

Thelma was tired and ready to go home. "Here's the short version: abysmal, wretched, bleak, and worst of all, godforsaken." The room went quiet.

"And you didn't slip him some of your medicinal home remedies? Something else you've got lurking in that bag of yours?" Sonny's bushy eyebrows were raised in a perfect arch.

"You are the most suspicious man I think I've ever met, Officer Simpson. No, I didn't slip him a drop of anything except a few grams of good old-fashioned wisdom."

There was nothing more to say. Finn thanked her for agreeing to come in and offered to find her a ride.

Sonny stood first and held out her coat. She slipped it on and patted his arms.

"Good muscle tone. You'll need it for the driveway."

CHAPTER FORTY-ONE

Mr. Groundhog promised an early spring, and he was right. The robins had returned and so had the geese, flying low in giant V-formations and honking to the world below that it was time to wake up and shake off those winter doldrums. Harper sat at her kitchen table and nursed a cup of coffee. She couldn't remember the last time she'd made one; she closed her eyes and inhaled the rich aroma. Maybe winter was behind her and it was time to shed those quiet colours.

She looked at her phone, let it go to sleep, and pressed it alive again. A message from Detective Yung flashed across the screen: *Call me.*

True drug himself into the room and landed in a chair. Harper took in his rumpled, slept-in clothing and the first signs of whiskers appearing on his upper lip. "Stop staying up so late."

"Midterms." He slotted two pieces of bread into the toaster. "Where's Sydney?" He stuck his head under the table.

"She's off making Valentine's Day cards with Mrs. Ryerson."

"Why so early?"

Harper pointed at the digital clock on the microwave. "It's 10:15 young man." She swatted his bottom. "You are behind your times."

The toast jumped from the toaster and so did Harper. She looked at her phone as the message flashed for a second time.

"Something important?" True continued buttering his toast and smeared it with a thick layer of Grandma Steele's raspberry jam.

Harper held it up for him to read. He sat down at the table and poured a glass of milk. Neither spoke. The phone lit up again. The detective was calling.

Harper answered on the next ring. "Good morning, Finn." She parted a handful of hair and let it fall across her face. Her responses were short: "Oh," or "I see," "Hmm," and ended with "Okay."

"Finish your breakfast. Detective Yung is on his way over." Harper poured her coffee down the drain, took the pot and emptied that too. She pulled on a coat and slipped out the back door.

****

At first Terri didn't notice the dark figure lingering by the side of her veranda, jacket zippered and hood pulled low. Harper spoke to the ground, "It's time, Terri. Can you come and bring Dallas with you?" She didn't wait for a response, just turned on her heels and retraced her steps back home.

Terri continued rocking in her favourite chair, imprinting the gentleness of the spring sun on her face and drawing strength from the earth beneath her feet. When she was ready, and not before, she tapped on the window to get Dallas's attention.

Inside the front closet, she retrieved a dry-cleaning pouch and pulled out a silk, lavender-coloured scarf. She draped the scarf about her neck. Fifteen years had vanished from her life, but not from her reflection in the hallway mirror—here, it had doubled.

****

Finn and Sonny sped towards Onyx Ave, climbed the steep grade up Greystone Boulevard, and rolled to a stop inside Rosewood Cul-de-sac, second house on the left. Harper met them at the door.

Finn gave a nod to the table. Sonny shuffled in behind; mentally counting chairs—not enough for everyone he calculated. "It's probably best if you deliver the news, Detective Yung." He snagged the last seat.

Harper opened the pantry door and pulled out a stool. "Here." She handed it to Finn. He removed his overcoat and laid it on the stool and held up an official-looking document. "As you know, the assessment period for Ng is over and the First City psychiatrist assigned to his case released her findings this morning." Terri held out her hand.

"Hold on," Sonny said. "There's more."

"More?" True grimaced.

Sonny spoke to Terri. "Detective Yung has *other* news."

She closed her eyes and inhaled. "Okay, I'm ready."

"Here you go." Finn handed the psych evaluation to Terri. She flipped to the last page: *Not Mentally Fit to Stand Trial.*

Dallas pulled her close. "And the *other* news?"

"Ng is dead. He died early this morning."

Terri's façade shattered and her bottom lip began to quiver. "I killed him."

Sonny pushed his chair back and stood beside Finn. "No, Miss Newman. What you did was self-defense and don't let that Moore kid tell you any different." He looped his thumbs through his suspenders.

Harper straightened her posture. "*That Moore kid?*" She searched her son's face for answers. "What does that mean?"

"Everett was using those videos to get himself into a film school in Toronto. The school probably has multiple copies."

"Multiple?" Terri sagged against Dallas.

True nodded. "Ben told me it's part of the admission requirements."

Sonny pulled out his phone. "Not for long." He stepped outside and placed a call.

"Hello, Miss Verna. I have a favour to ask: round up Mr. & Mrs. Moore, pronto. It's time we gave them a lesson on parenting." He smiled and waited for her to groan and say, *No, Simpson, I'm too busy.* "Let's call this payback for all the whiskey you poured down poor old Mrs. Ryerson's throat, and now every time it snows I'm the one she calls to shovel it for her!"

Harper was still mystified. "How on earth did you learn about the copies?"

Finn patted his notebook. "Mrs. Ryerson. Picture her as an enormous vat filled with information you couldn't imagine." He had recorded it all. Finn picked up his coat from the stool and slung it over his arm. "We wanted you to know firsthand—he can't hurt you anymore."

Harper followed him to the doorway and then called him back. "Finn?" Her breathing was raspy. "I . . . I was wondering if you'd like to join me for dinner, tomorrow, six p.m.? The kids are spending the night with their grandparents." She suddenly felt shy and awkward, not sure why she'd added the last part.

"He'd love to, Harper. Is there anything he can bring? He makes a fine haggis, if you're interested," Sonny shouted as Finn shoved him to the curb.

"Ignore him." He blushed. "Six p.m. is fine."

"And, thanks, but no thanks for the offer of sheep guts." She laughed as she turned the doorknob—about to leave. "Just out of curiosity, detective, what is your favourite dish?"

"Me?" He whispered into her ear, "Not haggis." She laughed again and twirled her hair. Finn inhaled her beauty. She smelled like a field of wild flowers—raw and passionate, bursting with colour. She let him take her hand. "I'm a simple man, Harper. If you make it, I'll eat it, and I'll love it."

She stepped inside, a smile creeping into the chambers of her heart. "That'll do, detective. That'll do."

CHAPTER FORTY-TWO

After her baking partner had gone home to take her afternoon nap, Thelma finished cleaning the kitchen. She wrung the dishcloth and wiped the counters. Everything sparkled. She kept reliving the phone call from Harper: *It's a new day, Thelma. Ng is dead.*

She had plugged in the kettle to make a cup of Oolong tea when suddenly she was on top of her little footstool, reaching into the back of the cupboard where Abe had kept the *good stuff*. She pulled out a dusty bottle of Irish whiskey and brewed a pot of coffee instead.

With an Irish coffee in one hand and a picture of Quigley before her, Thelma pulled two documents from her purse and crumpled them. She reached for the poker and added a fresh log to her crackling fire.

"Here's to you, Quigley." She tossed the first page into the blaze and watched it ignite.

CHAPTER FORTY-THREE

Finn pulled into the Rouge Market Square and parked beside *Poison* Ivy's Laundry. He'd finally figured out his problem—starch. His shirts were a little less crisp now, but at least he had touchable skin. He placed his laundry ticket on the counter and waited while the mechanical track swung hundreds of items through the air. It stopped and Ivy pulled down his clean shirts.

"Hey, you look like a cat-kind-of-guy," she said. "You need a kitten." It was a statement, not a question.

She pulled a box from beneath the counter. It was full of domestic kittens. The one that caught his eye was a black and white long hair with pink pads and a pink nose. Finn bundled him into one palm.

"Have they had their shots?"

"Read the sign, buddy. It says *free* kittens, not kittens with shots. That part's up to you."

"What if they have distemper?"

Ivy snapped her fingers and held out a hand for the return of the kitten. Finn held tight. "There's a vet at the end of this strip mall." She pointed to the right. "Have him checked out. If he doesn't pass mustard, toss him in the dumpster. What do I care? I've got three more."

Finn grabbed his shirts and the cat and stormed out of the store.

"Works every time." She petted the remaining kittens before she tucked them back beneath the counter.

****

Finn threw his shirts into the car and steamed off to the vet's office. No sooner had he opened the door than the receptionist called out, "Doc, we've got another one."

The doc told Finn he was the third person Ivy had "convinced" to take a kitten. He relaxed, then smiled, then laughed out loud. The fur ball snuggled into his neck and purred.

"Come on little fella, let's get you checked out." The doc poked and prodded, took his temperature and listened to his heartbeat.

"He's a healthy one, but he needs his shots. Where's he going to live?"

"He's a gift for a friend." Finn told him. He shared details about an elderly woman who'd lost her cat and what a comfort a new kitten might be for her.

Something about Finn's description rattled the doc's memory. "Does she live on Onyx Ave?"

"Yes, she does. Why?"

"Oh, it's probably nothing—I just recall something from a few months back." The doc looked at Finn and noticed the Rundle PD badge clipped to his belt. "I'm sure it'd be okay to share this— one of the residents on Onyx Ave had a cat . . ."

Finn was two steps ahead of him. "Mrs. Ryerson?"

"Yes! Oh, I'm so glad you're acquainted." Finn nodded. "Then you also know that her cat, Quigley, was shot in early November."

"November 1ˢᵗ."

"Right again! You do know your facts."

"And her cat died from a gunshot."

"No, no." The doc corrected him. "It was a flesh wound. He had other complications."

Finn sat down on the small bench beside the examination table.

"His behaviour was . . . off-putting. That's the best way to describe it."

"Off-putting?"

"He was snarly and twitchy, wouldn't eat or drink, and, now that I recall, he was dragging his hind legs. That's when I suspected."

"Rabies?"

"No, but it's funny to hear you say that. Mrs. Ryerson stopped in just before Christmas and asked me the same thing. She was spellbound: wanted to know every detail about rabies. Like, what would happen if Quigley had infected someone before he died, and what would happen if the person didn't receive treatment in time—or at all! My goodness, she's a pistol." He laughed and adjusted his glasses. "But no, it wasn't rabies. It was diabetes and quite advanced, to the point his kidneys had shut down. Poor fellow. There was nothing we could do for him."

"And you verified this?"

The doc removed his glasses. "Naturally."

"And Mrs. Ryerson was aware of this?" The doc nodded again. "I guess I'm just confused about the vet bill you sent her."

The doc powered up his PC and checked Quigley's records. "That wasn't a bill; it was an estimate. She said she wanted to rule out all possible causes: things like feline leukemia—and, oh yes, I see here she had me tick the box for rabies."

"Wasn't the cat already dead?" Finn raised his eyebrows.

"Oh, yes, well over a month by that time—and cremated, to boot."

"So, how did you expect to run these tests?"

The doc hung his head. "She seemed desperate, hurting; I just wanted to help. I told her it was impossible to verify anything at this point. Plus, it made no sense—Quigley had always been up to date on his shots." The doc snickered as he remembered Quigley. "He may have acted like a rabid beast, but that was his personality: he was a natural-born sour puss."

Finn grinned. "So, you're admitting that a little, old lady strong-armed you into preparing that invoice, even though her cat was dead, and you had no earthly way to run the tests, even if you wanted to?"

Doc shrugged. "That pretty much sums it up."

Finn raised the fur ball to his face and nuzzled the kitten's nose. "Let's go see your new home."

****

The radio announcer was right on cue with a song from the seventies by Cat Stevens and his *Tea for the Tillerman* album. Finn meandered over to Thelma's house, the fur ball riding shot gun on his shoulder. He pulled into her driveway and juggled his way out of the car, balancing the fur ball with a bag of food and some kitten toys: three blind mice (stuffed, assorted colours), a catnip teddy bear, one purr pillow, and something called a *Hugga Wubba*—he had no idea what it did, but the receptionist assured him that the fur ball needed it.

Thelma's curtains fluttered and her front door swung wide. "What have we here, detective?"

"Finn. Please."

He held out his hand and released the four-ounce ball of joy into Thelma's outstretched palm. She pressed him to her cheek and kissed him. "Hello, Little Abner. I've been waiting for you." Thelma retrieved a folded piece of paper from her pocket.

"Finn, take this before I change my mind." She held it out. "Go on, now. I know for a fact you've got bigger plans than this tonight."

It was a signed confession from Ng. Finn skimmed through the details. "He died this morning, Thelma."

"Yes, yes, I know. From a brain aneurysm."

"How on earth did you learn that detail?"

She sighed. "Hospitals always contact *Next of Kin*. It's policy."

He smiled and held up the confession. "And, how did you get this?"

"Someone may or may not have persuaded him that he had rabies and was about to die a slow and tortured death." She refused to look at Finn. "Of course, that's hearsay. And I can't guarantee that rumour, or disclose my sources."

"And this *someone* may have offered him treatment if he would only confess?"

"That's how I understand it." The black-and-white fur ball purred and she giggled. "If that three-inch crater in his head hadn't done the trick, this letter might have."

"Remind me never to cross you."

She brushed the kitten's tail from her face. "You see, Little Abner? He understands. Yes, he does," she cooed. Thelma retreated into the house and shut the door. Finn picked his chin up off the ground and walked back to his car. Things suddenly made more sense and he tucked the note into his pocket. The letter would keep—forever—maybe, but definitely for tonight.

CHAPTER FORTY-FOUR

The early evening air was crisp and clean around the edges, perfect for love and new lovers. Harper shut the fridge and sighed. *It's too soon. No, it's too late.* A mini war raged in her brain. She pulled out her recipe book and dusted off the cover. "That's not a good sign."

She laughed out loud as her fingers traced over the old recipes she used to make for Reggie. They were still covered in drops of sauces and other assorted, mystery splatters—*and love*, she reminded herself.

Harper set out two crystal wine glasses, then uncorked a bottle of red wine to let it breathe. The table was arranged and music floated in from the living room. Now, all she had to do was wait. Wait for the sound of his vehicle, for the closing of his door, and for his knock at her door. *Or, would it be a gentle rap?* She turned her head to check the time and there he was—no knock at all. He'd brought flowers and set them on the counter. Harper smiled.

"First thing you should know is that I haven't cooked a thing." She was thirteen again, with knobby knees, braces on her teeth, and a scrunched-up nose.

Finn took her in his arms. "First thing you should know is that I didn't come here to eat."

Harper responded to an unspoken yearning. "You have no idea how long I've been waiting for you."

"Yes, I do." His lips trembled as he kissed the woman standing before him, his woman.

ABOUT THE AUTHOR

In 2007, Laureen entered a writing contest determined to submit her version of *The Old Man and the Sea*. The process of writing her heart and soul out for seventy-two hours straight, over a long weekend in September, reignited a passion for writing that had been vacationing for the better part of her life. It was a clarion call to share her stories with the world, or North America, or Canada, or Alberta, or Central Alberta, or Lacombe, or family, or friends, or Calvin, or Lulu— She is thrilled to give her stories wings; her heart soars with delight for them.

Laureen makes her home in Lacombe, Alberta, Canada, with her husband, Calvin, and their adorable pug, Lulu.

If you have a comment you'd like to share, she may be reached at:
www.blwpub.shaw.ca

www.ingramcontent.com/pod-product-compliance
Lightning Source LLC
Chambersburg PA
CBHW051953170626
46808CB00007B/2600